William Horton

Memoir of the late Thomas Scatcherd

A family record

William Horton

Memoir of the late Thomas Scatcherd
A family record

ISBN/EAN: 9783337150563

Printed in Europe, USA, Canada, Australia, Japan

Cover: Foto ©Raphael Reischuk / pixelio.de

More available books at **www.hansebooks.com**

MEMOIR

OF THE LATE

THOMAS SCATCHERD

*BARRISTER-AT-LAW, QUEEN'S COUNSEL, AND MEMBER OF
PARLIAMENT FOR THE NORTH RIDING OF
MIDDLESEX, CANADA.*

A FAMILY RECORD.

By WILLIAM HORTON, Esq.

BARRISTER-AT-LAW.

PREFACE.

WHEN a man is suddenly cut down in the prime of his life and usefulness, and is followed to the grave by thousands of mourners, the event naturally awakens a desire to know something of his personal qualities and connection with public affairs.

It is intended in this Memoir to briefly describe York-shire, home of the Scatcherd ancestry, and to present some prominent outlines from the life of the late THOMAS SCATCHERD. Also to present outlines of his paternal and maternal Grandfathers; his Father and Uncle Thomas; and, with these, mention incidents related to their early settlement in the country.

Should these pages take a wider range than may seem proper for a Memoir, it is because the relatives and inti-mate friends have been kept in view rather than the general reader. And further, with the thought that this book might be acceptable in form of a Family Record, it is presented as such to the family.

CONTENTS.

CHAPTER VII.

CHAPTER VIII.

CHAPTER IX.

CHAPTER X.

MEMOIR.

MEMOIR.

CHAPTER I.

Mr. Thomas Scatcherd, Merchant in Hull, England—Ancient Yorkshire—
Ancient Wyton.

THOMAS SCATCHERD, Barrister-at-Law, Queen's
Counsel, and Member of Parliament for the North
Riding of Middlesex, Dominion of Canada, was son of
John Scatcherd, Justice of the Peace, Warden of the
County, and Member of Parliament for the West Riding
of Middlesex.

John was son of Thomas Scatcherd, a merchant of
Hull, Yorkshire, England, political associate and financial
supporter of William Wilberforce in parliamentary elections, and in the many good works which promoted
public morality, free institutions and human well-being—
good works which, through nearly half a century, made
that one unofficial Yorkshire member a parliamentary
power, with a name still surviving, still illustrious; and
which, with other public services, and personal virtues
eminently his own, keeps the name of Thomas Scatcherd,

2

merchant of Hull, pleasingly fresh in the civic records of
that town. Two overflowing rivers, Humber and Hull,
confined within embankments; docks constructed for
largest shipping; largest ships built; Baltic timber trade
greatly expanded; the Greenland whale fishery raised
from small ventures to a national industry and commer-
cially centralized in the river Humber; the importation
of Swedish iron made a staple trade to supply wants in
the mechanical arts, for which British iron was not at the
time suitable—these were some of the local enterprises
which Hull bankers and merchants undertook in years
when the grandfather of the subject of this Memoir was
among them, an adviser and enlivening leader. In relation to national affairs, his correspondence and personal
intimacy with distinguished public men—adverted to
more in detail presently—shows that, in addition to a
pleasing record in the municipality of Hull, the memory
of this Yorkshire merchant belongs to the annals of
English patriotism. The influence of his moral life is
inherited by descendants.

The coat of arms borne by the Scatcherds of Yorkshire
and their descendants resident in Canada, and in the
United States, is a stag proper, indicating an independent
social condition in the feudal ages. The king was to
them the Lord Paramount, their heritage lying in the
territory of Deira—"Land of Deer." This Land of
Deer comprised the counties of York, Durham, North-

umberland, south of Tweed river, and parts of the
counties of Berwick, Haddington and Edinburgh, north
of Tweed. Edwin of Deira is reputed to have built
Edinburgh Castle, giving his name to the city. A greater
work was the Christian baptism of himself, family and
people.

Another coat of arms borne by Mr. Thomas Scatcherd
of Hull, on sets of rich China ware, and on a baptismal
font, was a raised arm, outstretched, grasping a naked
scimeter. Under alternate shadows and lustrous lights
ecclesiastical, around the Minster of St. John of Beverley, the Scatcherd ancestry drew swords in defense of
country and king—civic borough charter and charter
of the Church.

At other times they took joy in the forests of Deira,
hunting the stag. Hence the heraldic bearings.

The physical elements of Yorkshire and its wide limits
have physiologically and industrially given a special character to the inhabitants. In geology the county is an
epitome of England, Wales and Scotland. All the common metals and coal fields are represented. The ocean
washes the east. The navigable rivers, Humber, Hull
and Ouse, flow at the south. The Tees at north, with
Durham and Northumberland coal fields in proximity.
A surface of hill, dale, plain and marsh measures five
thousand nine hundred and eighty-three square miles.
That area was peopled in 1851 by one million seven

hundred and ninety-seven thousand nine hundred and
ninety-five inhabitants; increased to over two millions in
1878. Previous to the Reform Act of 1832, the parliamentary electors of that wide county were conveyed to
vote at the Castle Yard in York city, many of them at
cost of rival candidates, the poll being open three weeks.
This explains both the great expense of a Yorkshire
contested election and its influence on national opinion.
The self-abnegation of voters who, refusing such convey-
ance, and having none of their own, walked to York to
vote, forty, fifty, sixty miles, proved the moral integrity
of a goodly proportion of thinking Yorkshiremen. The
generous amounts of money subscribed by wealthier
freeholders, such as Thomas Scatcherd of Hull, to save a
candidate from pecuniary ruin, was another characteristic
of the great county.

But in respect of Yorkshire influence it may be said
that through most of the centuries, perhaps all since
A. D. 71, the men and women of that land lying between
the Humber and the Tweed, south and north; the ocean
and the hills, east and west, have imparted to the other
sections of Britain a tone and bias of thought. Let their
historic shadows flit before us a minute. Dimly, indis-
tinctly, they can only now be discerned. Yet through
those fragments of a long-ago life Imperial Colonial
Canada may obtain a glimpse of the British Empire in
its cradle. And republican America, eldest daughter of

England, beautiful runaway bride, well wedded now,
proudly independent,—she perchance may listen to the
long-ago lisping of her mother's mother tongue.

When the Roman general, Agricola, A. D. 71, penetrated into the country which is now Yorkshire, Durham,
and Northumberland, the land was inhabited by the
Brigantes, the most powerful of British tribes, according
to Tacitus, son-in-law of Agricola. Roman roads were
constructed in direct lines up hill and down, through
marshes, and over streams; a union of several being
made at suitable eminences near the banks of the larger
rivers, as at Eboracum—York. The Roman road by
Watling street, in the city of London, is still traceable
in this nineteenth century through the parish of Isling-
ton. At Battle Bridge, site of the Great Northern
Railway Depot in London, Queen Boadicea, personally
leading a British force, attacked the Romans, A. D. 61,
but was defeated; thirty thousand of her faithful people
slain, and herself atrociously put to death.

Agricola made treaties with the Brigantes, dissuading
them from misuse of their fertile lands as mere hunting
grounds. He taught them a way to wealth by digging
ditches around marshy soils. He taught the arts of
plowing, sowing of seeds, and harvesting; introducing
new vegetables and fruits. The domestication of fowls,
and breeding of sheep were exemplified; also improved
methods of preparing, spinning, and weaving wool for

clothing. And from that time, in the country which is modern Yorkshire, the manufacture of woolen cloth has been, less or more, a distinctive industry. In the West Riding the quantities of woolens, linens, cutlery and mill machinery produced annually in this nineteeth century, are, in variety, commercial value and world-wide diffusion, marvelous; exceeding the grandest fancy flights of poets or magicians.

The Brigantes were teachable, and more, they were grateful. They named the arts of plowing, seed-sowing, and harvesting, Agricola-culture. This was colloquially shortened to Agriculture. Roman men and Brigantine maidens loved and lived in happy matrimony; the Cæsarean nose in their posterity bearing witness.

When the legions of Rome finally left Britain, A. D. 420, the physically vigorous, intellectual offspring remained. They took pride in burring the letter r as the Romans did. To this day the Northumbrian peasantry of the fields, and towns-people of Berwick-on-Tweed, burr in manner of Mark Antony's whispers to Cleopatra, when the very winds upon the Nile were love-sick.

The Brigantes, under the prosperity which agriculture and wool-weaving conferred, neglected their warrior training, and frontier forts. Their wealth allured the Picts, Scots, and Highland Caledonians. The Picts (correctly Pechs) were a race of strong men, short in the lower limbs, short in body, but with arms long and

muscular. They wielded oaken and hazel cudgels on
battle-fields, rushing into close quarters with the archers
who shot with bows and arrows, breaking their limbs;
leaving them literally not a leg to stand upon. In building walls of cities and castles, the Pechs formed lines of
men, miles long, standing shoulder to shoulder up acclivities, down ravines, across marshes, passing stones one to
another.

After the Scoto-Irish the Caledonians and the Pechs
had invaded and plundered the Brigantes, the Saxons
came over the sea, from an opposite direction. For sake
of the prolific lands the Saxons not only plundered the
agricultural wool-workers, but slew them. Such as
escaped fled, for a time, to the mountains of Wales.
At the Druidical British temple on Salisbury Plain, the
mysterious astronomical stones still surviving and known
to fame as Stonehenge, a vast concourse of midnight
moonlight worshipers were slain as idolators by Saxon
adorers of the god Wodin. But murder was done more
probably for love of the new land, than through abhor-
rence of the old worship. Changes in religious systems
have not extinguished in Wiltshire the transmitted in-
stincts of Moon-worship. The people all up through the
Christian centuries continued to assemble, and still they
gather in the light of Luna around the olden altars of
Stonehenge. They are called Moon-rakers now-a-days.

Saxon policy changed the names of places, so far as a new orthography might promote change. One British term for a river was Yar, Ayr, Aire, Ewer, Ure, as variously spelt by their successors. The Ure river, subsequently by the Saxons named Ouse, flowed out of valleys among the western hills, and washed the walls of the old Roman fort, Eboracum. The Saxon effort to confer a new name on that Roman fortress and on Brigantine territory resulted in this orthography: "Eurewicscire." The " Eurewic" became converted to York; and the "scire" to shire. Thus from Wic, or Wick, or Wyke, a bailiff's district, and scire, a sheriff's district, England got her York and Yorkshire; America its New York; and Canada its " Little Muddy York," now transformed to the beautiful city of Toronto. The East, West, and North Ridings of Yorkshire came from the "Thirdings;" locally pronounced, " Tridings."

The landing of Ida, the Angle, and his tribal followers, began a lingual epoch. They came from the shores of the Baltic sea. The name of this tribe took root and life, in land and in language; growing from Yorkshire where the Angles stepped ashore, climbing the steep ascent, to Anglo-land, and England. Growing and ripening to the English and Anglo-Saxon language. To Anglo-Saxon races of fair women and brave men. To Old England, and out of that to the New England of America. To the ever-widening diffusion, the world over, of

the language which governs international commerce and
the attendant civilizations; the language of the philosophy which gives free navigation to oceans; free institutions to political communities; and which promises to be
a missionary tongue to a universal Christianity. That paternal chieftain, Ida the Angle, gave first utterance on
English soil to the tongue of the world's destinies at
Flamboro Head, Yorkshire, A. D. 547.

Ida settled with his people between the rivers Tees
and Tyne, and founded the kingdom of Bernicia. In 617
the Angles of Bernicia and Brigantes of Deira united,
and were called Northumbrians.

Edilfrid, King of Northumbria, being slain in 621,
Edwin of Deira succeeded; and a few years later, was
styled Rex Anglorum.

Presently, in tracing the conflicts of the human intel-
lect, struggling in the night-time of its natural religion
to find the Deity, Edwin re-appears. And with him,
Wyton;—home of the Scatcherds.

Thomas Scatcherd, the Hull merchant, was born in the
town of Beverley, eighteen miles northwest of Hull, in
the year 1750. Beverley was enfranchised as a royal
free borough, and its grand Minster built and dedicated
to St. John, by King Athelstane, A. D. 925. The place
was named from the " Beaver lacs," small sheets of water
in the Holderness marsh, fed by springs from the lower
margins of the wolds; the wolds extending to York city,

thirty-five miles westerly; the marshes eighteen miles easterly and south to Hull. In early centuries of semi-civilization, in a sparsely peopled country, that admirable engineer, the beaver, abounded in the Holderness marshes of Yorkshire, as it did twelve hundred years later in the running streams of Nissouri township, Upper Canada. In this township the sons of Mr. Scatcherd, of Hull, penetrated the forest in vicinity of Beaver Dams, making farms and homesteads in the western wilderness, equal in beauty and abundant harvests to any in England. A renewal of renown to the name of Agricola, and to the Northumbrian Agricola-culture.

The marshes of the Holderness district were drained, and became the pasture-lands on which Flemish cows, imported to Hull from Flanders, were mated in English herds; producing the bovine parents of the deep-bodied, level-backed, short-horned progeny called Durhams.

Within the Minster at Beverley, the book-reading boy, Thomas Scatcherd, saw on many occasions the two pictured figures of King Athelstane, founder of the Church; and St. John of Beverley, patron and protector of Church and town. And he read in quaint orthography this couplet between the king and the saint:

> " Als free, make I thee ;
> As hert can thynk, or eyh can see."

The event which induced the building and endowment of Beverley Minster, and inspired Athelstane in a season

of personal gladness and local rejoicing, to grant Beverley
borough a charter exceptionally liberal, freeing the town
from tolls and taxes, and other burdens of feudal servi-
tude; conferring on it free lands, and within certain limits, free hunting of deer,—that event was one of a long
series imprinted in the public memory, sung in ballads,
told in story, and read of in books. It was the battle of
the Brunen Burh. Water-springs issuing from the Yorkshire wolds (otherwise wool-lands or sheep pastures), outside the town, were in Saxon the " Brunen," and " Burh,"
the town.

Athelstane had penetrated Scotland as far as a colony
of ancient Britons in the vale of Clyde. A confederate
force of Caledonians, Pechs, Scoto-Irish, Norwegians and
Danes, led by the renowned Olaf of Norway, followed
Athelstane into England by land, and partly by sea to
the Humber. The two armies met at the Brunen Burh
of Beverley. A sanguinary battle was fought. The
English, victorious, drove the Danes to their ships, and
the Caledonians to their mountains, slaying many thousands. Then arose the grand structure, Beverley Minster, and the people sang the heroic ballad of Brunen
Burh.

From Beverley and school Thomas Scatcherd, with a
mercantile career before him, proceeded to Hull. This
town is situated beside the estuary of the Humber, at
mouth of the smaller river Hull, anciently the river

Wyke. Distance from London, 183 miles north; from
York, 53 miles east.

Separating the counties of York and Lincoln, the
Humber also unites them by its ferries. Over the water
by ferry, or private boat when more agreeable, Robert
Wilberforce, a Hull merchant, went to Barton in Lincolnshire, to have joy in the presence of his future bride,
daughter of Thomas Bird and his wife. The elder members of the Bird and Wilberforce families became friends,
and the younger members associates of Thomas Scatcherd. He in turn assisted in leading the youthful William
Wilberforce to the political steps of his public eminence.

In the early surveys of Upper Canada a prevailing
nomenclature of townships came with Governor Simcoe
and his assistants from old Lincolnshire and adjacent
parts of the Land of Deira. From that land came Beverley, Scarboro and York. From the shire of Lincoln
came Saltfleet, Grimsby, Welland, and twenty more.
And the name of Barton came, the township in which
Hamilton city lies, head reposing on the mountain slopes,
feet dipping in the water of Ontario—lake of the sun's
love.

And from vicinity of the town which for six hundred
years has been called Hull, came the name of a village
to Upper Canada, to the township of Nissouri, which in
English history is associated with holiest aspirations of
the soul, profoundest of the mysteries of God,—the

advent of the Gospel of Jesus Christ. The place is
Wyton. It was anciently dedicated to the uses of two
or more heathen temples. British Druids assembled
there on a grassy eminence, geologically a drift of gravel,
covered with the mold and verdure of ages. They kin-
dled there the fires of Bel. Midsummer morn was
watchfully awaited, and the rising sun adored as soon as
the earliest gleam of the glowing god was discerned on
the ocean out by Spurn Head.

Romans came with a new religion, overthrowing the
altars of Bel, burning the groves of oak trees, holly trees
and mistletoe boughs; building a temple, and erecting
therein or around it the statues and images of Grecian,
Phœnician and Chaldean astronomical deities. Scandinavian mariners came, and, contemptuously deriding
Roman and British mythological statues, erected the
altars and images of their own Thor and Freya, both
inherited out of deep oriental Aryan antiquity. Suc-
ceeding the earlier of the Scandinavian mariners came
the Saxons. They erected altars to Wodin. The Angles
next arrived, tolerant of Thor, Freya, Wodin, Jupiter,
Juno, or the Bel-fires and mistletoe boughs, conditionally
with their own Elfins, Mannikins and Water Kelpies. Of
all these, Thor was at once the most terrible, most
dreaded and most generally accepted. The altars of
Thor, or their name, may be traced on a hundred hills
within the British Islands at this day, where the prefix or

termination, Tor, still adheres. Also, at Gibraltar, the olden Gibel-Tor of Scandinavian mariners sailing to the Mediterranean, and there trading with the Moors of Spain and Morocco. Also, in the word tariff; merchant mariners, having paid customs taxes to the Moors at Tariffa in Spain, charged them to merchants at home as Tariffa dues—"Tor," place of worship; "Iffa," diminutive and feminine for the lesser Tor, near to the greater Gibel-Tor.

Into the country of Deira, at the temple of pagan idolatry, came Paulinas, a missionary, preaching the Gospel of Jesus Christ. He taught that the true God is a God of love, not a demon like the diabolical Thor; that Christ, the redeemer of souls and purifier of moral life, was the spiritual emanation of God's love; that repentance for sins committed, renunciation of willful immoralities, and faithful service of this, the true God, would bring peace of mind at the hour of death, and secure for the departing soul a life everlasting in heaven, transcendently glorious, unspeakably happy.

Edwin, King of Deira, listened to Paulinas. A brotherhood and sisterhood of love in this life would be much to gain from confession of belief and Christian baptism. Yet brotherly and sisterly love were conditions for this life only; peace and good will among nations, offered by Paulinas in name of the Gospel, depended on the peacefulness of national neighbors. But the life of bliss everlasting, what a prize to win! Belief in the sanctifying efficacy of baptism and the eucharist; belief in the divine nature and mission of Jesus; repentance for evil actions done and renunciation of every willful wickedness in the future,—these were the terms for the prize of the high calling to this offer of a happy eternity. And the very acceptance of the terms was happiness, even in this life. How beneficent, excellent, beautiful the religion of the Gospel of Jesus Christ!

Edwin summoned the Witanmote, a Parliament of Wise Men. This council of wisdom assembled in or about the year A. D. 625, within the hall of the Roman Delgovitia, formerly the Brito-Brigantine sacred grove of the Druids, Delgwe.

Camden, following for authority the Saxon ecclesiastical historian, The Venerable Bede, wrote thus:

"And in a little village not far off there stood a temple of idols, which was in very great honor, even in Saxon times; and, from the heathen gods in it, was then called God-mundingham, and now, in the same sense, Godmanham. There, where Wighton, a small village well stocked with husbandmen now stands, upon the small river Hullness, Edwin of Deira declared his conversion to Christianity."

The Wise Men being assembled, the unlooked-for incident of a sparrow flying into the hall through an open doorway, fluttering there a minute, then out at the opposite doorway, gave a philosophic thinker of Edwin's council a theme for illustration. He spoke:

"The present life of man, O King, seems to me in comparison of that time which is unknown to us, like to the sparrow swiftly flying through this room, well warmed with the fire made in midst of it, wherein you sit at supper in the winter with commanders and ministers, whilst the storms of rain and snow prevail abroad; the sparrow, I say, flying in at one door, and immediately out at another, is not while within affected with the winter storm; but after a very brief interval of what is to him fair weather and safety, he vanishes out of your sight, returning from one winter to another. So this life of man appears for a moment; but of what went before, or what is to follow, we are ignorant. If, therefore, this new doctrine contains something more certain, it seems justly deserving to be followed."

Bede gave the tradition, including the actual inflight and outflight of the bird. The incident was natural, possible and probable.

In the year 1874, when clergymen of the English Episcopal Church in Canada were assembled in the city of Ottawa, to inquire and decide about the truth, or untruth, of circumstances affecting the congregation and minister of one of the Ottawa English churches, a white dove flew in at the open window, and alighting on the shoulder of the clerical gentleman principally concerned, sat there

a few moments; then, fluttering around his head, took
wing and away by the window where it entered. None
there knew more of that white dove than is here told.
The incident came to the *Church Herald* in Toronto, an
item in general church news.

The inflight and outflight of the sparrow at Wyton in
presence of Edwin, King of Deira, was no doubt a natural incident also. The memory of the occurrence lasts,
and charms, by the aptitude of the councilor's illustration of the two eternities—that past and that to
come. "If, therefore," said Edwin's Wise Councilor,
"this new doctrine contains something more certain [than
chance at one doorway of life and utter darkness at the
other] it seems justly to deserve to be followed."

Edwin, the king, arising from the throne and uncover-
ing his head in honor of the Majesty of the God of
Heaven, and of the Son of God, Saviour of souls, spoke
standing, where otherwise he would have sat as a king
with head covered :

"Who of this assembled Council," he cried, "shall first
take courage to desecrate the temple of the idols, which
hitherto we have worshiped, but no longer believe in?"

Coifi, chief priest of the heathen temple, who had
already spoken, and declared for the doctrines of the
Gospel of Christ, stood up, and to the King and Council
opened his lips :

3

" I," said Coifi, " for who can more properly than myself destroy those things that I worshiped through igno-
rance? I do it as an example to others through the
wisdom given me by the true God."

Says a modern English historian:

" The altars and images which the priests of Northumbria overthrew have left no monuments in the land.
They were not built like the Druidical temples, under the
impulses of a great system of faith which, dark as it was,
had its foundation in spiritual aspirations. The pagan
worship which the Saxons brought to this land, was
chiefly cultivated under its sensual aspects. The Valhalla,
or heaven of the brave, was a heaven of fighting and
feasting, of full meals of boar's flesh and large draughts
of mead. Such a future called not for solemn temples,
and altars where the lowly and the weak might kneel in
the belief that there was a heaven for them, as well as for
the mighty in battle."

This is true of the absence of monumental structures.
No ruin is preserved of the idol temple overthrown by
Coifi and people of Deira baptized by Paulinas. But the
village built upon or near to the ground where Edwin and
Coifi accepted Christianity, has been memorable ever since
the day of the sparrow and the Wise Man's speech—the
day of the king's Christian baptism. It is cherished as
a spot of ground to love, with a name to be revered.
From it to Hull and return, Thomas Scatcherd took

pleasure in riding on his favorite gray horse. The name was affectionately brought to Canada by his son John.

In the year 1296, Edward I., from pious sentiments when informed of the memorable Christian event, prevailed upon the Lord of the Manor, the Abbot of Meaux, and other proprietors sprung from the Norman Conquest, to sell to him the lordship of Wyton with the town of Wyke. To Wyke the king gave a charter of incorporation, changing the name to Hull.

On twenty-fourth of August, 1759, William Wilberforce was born in Hull. He was a feeble infant, but grew in boyhood to be the admiration of companions, both in physical and mental vivacity. Left fatherless when aged nine, he was sent to Wimbledon near London, to be cared for by his uncle Samuel, brother of his father, a wealthy gentleman who, dying soon after, left to William a fortune, and the Wimbledon mansion, ·lands and gardens. With his widowed aunt the boy attended the assemblies who listened to the great preacher Whitfield. Removing to a school at Nottingham, and in due time going to the University of Cambridge, the religious impressions derived from the eloquent Methodist preacher and his aunt were, for a time, effaced. But after a season of gaiety among fellow-students in Cambridge, conscience became awakened. In 1776, he separated from riotous associates, choosing for confidential friend William Pitt, a fellow-student, Premier of England in after years.

At the age of fourteen, Wilberforce wrote and caused
to be published, in a city of York newspaper, a letter of
protestation against the trade in negro slaves. This subject gave character to the whole of his subsequent life.
It was one of the many subjects related to human well-
being and political justice, which began about that time
to exalt the moral reputation of England; to characterize
the county of York somewhat specially, and the town of
Hull pre-eminently.

In 1780, a vacancy occurred in the parliamentary representation of Hull. William Wilberforce, aged a few
weeks over twenty-one, was elected. Being a native of
the town, his personal qualities were known. A good
voice, fluent elocution, aptitude in the recital of anecdotes, comely countenance, generosity to the poor, absti-
nence from social excesses, reputation for practical piety
acquired amidst the university jollity then prevalent,—
those favorable attributes made young Wilberforce the
choice of the leaders of public thought.

In December, 1783, William Pitt was Prime Minister,
and Parliament dissolved. A place in the Cabinet was
offered to Wilberforce; but the Premier being like himself very young, the member for Hull declined office to
avoid unpopularity for the Government. The dissolution
of a Whig and Tory coalition had been effected, as well
as a dissolution of Parliament. Wilberforce warmly supported Pitt. From London he hastened to York city to

address a meeting of freeholders which had been summoned to sustain the late coalition and oppose the parti-
sans of the new ministry. In the midst of an emphatic
speech which carried the listeners, voices were heard
calling: " We'll have this man to be our county member." They had him; and before any of the contested
elections were advanced beyond a day or two in the
three weeks of polling, Wilberforce was elected by acclamation as one of the two members for Yorkshire. That
return led national opinion; and Government obtained a
majority.

In the earlier years of Pitt's ministry, Wilberforce,
assisted by his friends in Hull, prominent among whom
was Thomas Scatcherd, introduced a bill for parliamentary reform in Yorkshire. He proposed to give that
county additional members; several polling-places instead
of one; and to shorten the contest from three weeks to
three days. Pitt had previously introduced a reform
bill, but withdrew it. So did Wilberforce withdraw his
proposition, shrinking before the opposition raised against
it. But, strengthened by influential supporters at Hull,
and by their associates in Yorkshire, Wilberforce obtained in 1787 a royal proclamation, willingly acceded
to by the pious King George III., lamenting the preva-
lence of vice and immorality, and paternally enjoining on
leaders of society especially, and people generally, an
improvement in morals; a more faithful observance of

religious ordinances, and of Sunday, day of worship and of rest.

The sentiments of Thomas Scatcherd in the years of war between England and France, from the outbreak of hostilities in 1792, may be inferred from letters of correspondents and from his personal friendships.

In 1801, after a series of bad harvests, excessive prices of food, suspension of specie payments at the Bank of England from 1797, and a few military mistakes, though enlivened by some great naval victories, the nation joyously welcomed the negotiations for peace. The Mayor of Hull presented to this representative townsman an arm chair, with engraved silver plate, as a memorial of the return of "Peace and Plenty." The chair is now in Canada, at Wyton, township of Nissouri, in possession of his son Thomas Scatcherd. The silver tablet bears this inscription:

"Presented to Thomas Scatcherd by William Jarret, Esq., Mayor, in Memory of Peace and Plenty. Hull, Oct. 12, 1801.

MAY.	£	s.	d.	NOVEMBER.	£	s.	d.
Wheat, per quarter, . .	7	0	0	Wheat, per quarter, . .	3	3	0
Beef, per lb., ...	0	0	10	Beef, per lb., ...	0	0	6
Mutton, per lb., . . .	0	0	9	Mutton, per lb., . . .	0	0	6
Potatoes, per lb., . . .	0	1	4	Potatoes, per lb., . . .	0	0	4

In addition to the influence of the treaty of peace, the weather in 1801 had been favorable, and harvest abundant, compared with the harvests of three previous seasons; long remembered as "The Dear Years."

War was resumed in 1803. Napoleon had been elected First Consul of France for life. In all but name the Consul was sovereign. He was not willing to lose dominions won by the sword, and equivocally affected by the recent treaty. The projected invasion of England; the detention of English travelers as prisoners of war in France, and the successive defeats of Austrian and Prussian armies, gave a unity of thought to all Englishmen in the matter of national defenses, though divided in opinion as to the fitness of statesmen for their several offices. Addington succeeded Pitt in 1801; Pitt returned to power in 1805. His colleague, Lord Melville, Treasurer of the Navy in previous years, was impeached by the House of Commons on a charge of malversation. For this impeachment Wilberforce voted against his former friends. William Pitt retired, dying, as popularly said, of a broken heart. The Whig and Tory coalition cabinet of "All the Talents," under Lord Grenville, held office in 1806-7; and the most memorable of Yorkshire elections ensued.

Wilberforce had for twenty years led an agitation to extinguish the negro slave trade in so far as Great Britain shared it. He was now the independent candidate. Mr. Lascelles, the Tory, was son of a West India proprietor of sugar estates and slaves, and fifteen years the col-

league of Wilberforce as second member for Yorkshire.
The Whig candidate was Lord Milton, son of Earl Fitzwilliam. It being known that the Grenville ministry intended to lay before Parliament a bill to abolish the
slave trade, the whole slave-trading interests of Britain
were allied in support of Lascelles. It was known Lord
Milton, if elected, would support the Government measure for abolition. Tories who had long supported Wilberforce because he generally voted with Pitt, were supposed to be now alienated because of the vote on the
Melville impeachment. The adherents of Lascelles, and
of Milton, respectively, opened the conflict, conveying
their voters from all parts of the five thousand nine hundred and eighty-three square miles of Yorkshire, to the
Castle Yard in the city of York. In name of travel-
ing costs the Tory and Whig committees expended in
fifteen days all the money at their command, one hundred thousand pounds sterling each. The election lasted
three weeks. The first three days Wilberforce was lowest
on the poll. He had publicly said that his object in
seeking a seat in Parliament was to support measures of
general usefulness, and one especially which concerned
human well-being and the honor of Christian nations.
But he hesitated to believe that going to Parliament
with a ruined fortune, would promote such objects. His
friends in Hull subscribed money for costs strictly legiti-
mate. They enjoined on voters to give Wilberforce

plumpers until his name headed the poll; afterward the voters to prefer Wilberforce and Milton. At the end of fifteen days those two candidates showed so well ahead that the Lascelles party ceased to collect more voters.

Mr. W. J. Denison to Mr. Scatcherd.

This letter, without date other than "London, Monday," refers to the contested Yorkshire election of 1807.

Dear Scatcherd: I have paired off with Mr. Bethell, the chairman of Lascelles' committee at the British Coffee House.

I have worked like a horse, and flatter myself I have done more good among the city people (non-resident Yorkshire voters) than if I had gone down. Our meeting on Saturday evening was highly respectable.

It will half break my heart if we are beat.

Yours ever, affectionately,

W. J. DENISON.

Subscriptions in money to defray costs incurred for Wilberforce came to the committee from most parts of England and from Edinburgh. Scottish Glasgow, like English Bristol and Liverpool, was interested in the slave trade and West India produce; the merchants of those places subscribed for Lascelles.

At close of the poll in York city, Mr. Wilberforce visited Hull. In his diary the words are: "I was especially indebted to my old friends in Hull." He went first to Mr. Scatcherd, who, at his office, received the visitor's warm hand-shaking and congratulations for the eminently influential services rendered in the great contest.

A few passages quoted from correspondents writing to Mr. Scatcherd in those years, reveal sentiments common to them all in the matter of European disturbance under Napoleon's victories. The following from Mr. W. J. Denison, of London, one of a well-known Yorkshire family, unfolds not alone the sentiment of patriotism common to good Englishmen, but a specialty of his friend not so common:

[Extract.] *Dear Scatcherd:* I am much obliged to you for the turkey; still more for your kindness to Mrs. Sjostedt. She does not know how to express her gratitude to you and your family, and says, with tears, you are the best friend she ever had. * * *

What sad news from the continent. Where is it all to end?

LONDON, *28th November, 1806.*

A single sentence of history may tell what were the sad news from the continent: " Prussians irretrievably ruined at the battle of Jena; fortress after fortress surrendered to Napoleon, and the unfortunate king, stript of the greater part of his dominions, had no hope but in the assistance of Russia."

The kindness rendered Mrs. Sjostedt, a foreign lady
landed at Hull, and desiring to reach London, was an
advance of twenty guineas, on her own credibility, and
domestic hospitality at Wyton, the family residence.

Mr. Clarke, East India House, London, to Mr. Scatcherd.

EAST INDIA HO., *Oct. 24, 1808.*

Dear Sir : On Sunday, the 2d instant, I experienced
your liberality in the form of two brace of partridge, and
a very fine hare. They were all excellent, and came in
good condition, for which we thank you. * * *

Really, I do not see any likelihood of our prospects
brightening. That convention must be fully investigated.
British valour never shone brighter. The convention certainly has shaded it in a disgraceful manner. I think
with you the people at Hull have forgot themselves ; but
they want an able instructor, and when you left them
their good judgment, etc., etc., seems to have retired
also, but I hope not irretrievably. The convention was
a d–mn–d bad business. I beg you will excuse haste, as
I am at present engaged officially with several persons.
Accept our united thanks for your numerous favours, and
believe me to remain, with respect and gratitude, dear
sir, your much obliged and most humble servant,

A. CLARKE.

N. B. Our respectful compliments, with every good
wish, to Miss S., yourself and family.

The convention referred to so indignantly was an agreement known as the Convention of Cintra, signed by two British generals, Dalrymple and Burrard, subsequent to the battle of Vimeira, successfully fought and won, twenty-first August, 1808, under Sir Arthur Wellesley (afterwards Duke of Wellington). Wellesley had previously defeated the French in the battle of Rolica on the seventeenth, having only landed with his army in Portugal on first of the month. The British nation were enthusiastic at the reported uprising of Spanish and Portuguese people against a French invasion; and all but a section of opposition Whigs and some of their adherents, as at Hull, approved and urged the British intervention. The army under Wellesley had begun valliantly, but he was superseded by arrival from England, first of Burrard, next of Dalrymple, to the command in chief. A Russian fleet lay in the Tagus. The Convention of Cintra provided for the security of this fleet, and for the unmolested transport of the French army to ports in France. The English admiral, Sir Charles Cotton, refused assent to the convention in respect of the Russian fleet. It was captured, conditionally, to be restored to its own country six months after a conclusion of peace. Portugal by that arrangement being cleared of the French, Sir John Moore, who had been appointed chief in command, was directed by home authority to assail the French in northern Spain.

In that campaign, closing with the battle of Corunna
and death of the commander, January, 1809, Mr. James
N. Scatcherd, son of Mr. Scatcherd of Hull, served as a
commissioned officer, dying of hard service in campaign
and combat the following year.

Colonel Wardle to Mr. Scatcherd.

LONDON, ——— *1809.*

Sir : I have to thank you sincerely for the very handsome manner in which you are pleased to express yourself
upon my conduct respecting H. R. H. the Duke of York,
our late commander-in-chief. To be possessed of the
confidence and support of those who are the real friends
of their country is the utmost of my ambition. Amongst
that number I am sure your name will ever be enrolled ;
and I trust a determined opposition to corruption, let it
appear where or in what form it may, will continue to me
your good opinion and approbation. Mr. Maskew has
forwarded the haunch of venison you are kind enough to
send me ; and I shall certainly, as you wish, invite Lord
Folkstone and Sir Francis Burdett to partake of it, when
we shall have pleasure in drinking your health.

I am, sir, your much obliged and obedient servant,

GEO. W. WARDLE.

The allegations against the Duke of York referred to
an irregular and corrupt sale of army commissions. A
committee of Parliament, led by Colonel Wardle, took
evidence on the subject. After a prolonged investigation,

a decision was given acquitting the duke personally, but leaving on him the imputation of negligence in permitting a certain member of his household to exercise undue influence among subordinates in the War Office Department. His Royal Highness, feeling himself not wholly absolved, resigned command of the army. The Lord Folkstone mentioned in the letter was then a leading Whig, afterwards the Earl of Radnor, politically a philosophical Radical. Sir Francis Burdett was M. P. for Westminster; Radical in early life; Conservative when the Reform Act of 1832 had accomplished the object he so long contended for. He was father of the Baroness Burdett Coutts, a lady who, possessing the revenues of a long-established bank, and inheritress of a fortune besides, clothes herself in the moral grandeur of trustee for humanity, promoting numberless good works, all of them utilitarian, moral, beneficent.

On the tenth of December, 1809, Mr. Scatcherd died at his residence near Hull. His sickness lasted but a few days. The latest of letters on public affairs, received by him and still preserved, was that just quoted. In the Hull *Rockingham Newspaper* of December 16th, an obituary was published. It is here reproduced:

"On Sunday last, died at Wyton, in Holderness, in the fifty-ninth year of his age, after an illness of only three days, Thomas Scatcherd, Esq., of this town.

"A man whose memory, we trust, will long be cherished in this town and neighborhood. If widely-extended benevolence, heartfelt hospitality, sound sense and honest principles can protect their owner from the oblivion of the grave, who can expect to live longer in the memory of their friends than honest Tom Scatcherd! Besides possessing these qualities in an eminent degree, he superadded that energy which was peculiarly calculated to give them their due effect. His benevolence never slept, and his happy witticisms, the natural effusion of a joyous soul, enlivened every society. His fine open countenance bespoke the good humor that dwelt within; melancholy and misanthropy fled at his approach.

"His patriotism partook of the general warmth of his character, and no exertions were ever wanting on his part to arm every hand and encourage every heart against our foreign enemy, or to detect and punish corruption at home.

"On the election of members of Parliament for this and the neighboring boroughs, Mr. Scatcherd's exertions were most conspicuous; and to his well-deserved popularity, the successive Whig representatives of this town have been greatly indebted for their election. With these qualities it is not surprising that his society was much sought after, and his connections widely extended in the upper as well as middle ranks of life.

"In politics he was warmly and steadily attached to those principles which have been supported and adorned by a Chatham, a Saville, a Fox and a Fitzwilliam. But it is not on the shifting ground of party politics that Mr. Scatcherd's character is to rest. It will find a more enduring basis in the many social virtues which endeared him to the large circle of his friends; in his hospitality, his charity, his parental affection; in the powerful faculties of his mind, and the kind feelings of his heart. He was buried at South Cave, and though his funeral was performed according to his own direction with great privacy, many of his friends attended, unbidden, to drop a tear over the grave."

Another writer, familiar with the history of the time in which this well-esteemed gentleman lived, has sketched his connection with contemporary men and events. Thus:—

"Thomas Scatcherd was a successful merchant, descended from an ancient Yorkshire family. Active and earnest in political life, he took a spirited part in the elections of his city and county; especially in those of the well remembered William Wilberforce, conspicuous type of sterling British philanthropy in his day, who devoted himself earnestly, both in and out of Parliament, to various benevolent projects; such as abolition of the slave trade; society for bettering the condition of the poor; improvement of the condition of children employed in cotton mills; the better observance of Sunday, and many other matters of a like nature. It was well said of him that, 'Not one nation, but the whole human family participated in the benefits he conferred on his fellow-men.' He was a man after Scatcherd's own heart and correctly reflected his principles, as was shown by the strenuous efforts made against corrupt influences which were so strong in the Yorkshire election of 1807 that the Tory pro-slavery candidate, Mr. Lascelles, and his party, expended £100,000 sterling to defeat him. A like sum being spent on behalf of the Whig anti-slavery candidate, Lord Milton, who stood in opposition to Lascelles; and £28,000 to secure the return of Mr. Wilberforce, who stood as independent. The united expenses at this election amounted to $1,140,000. From being lowest on the poll for some days, the influence of Mr. Scatcherd and his policy of inducing voters to give "plumpers" for the independent candidate, advanced Wilberforce to head of the poll.

" Few, if any, residents in Hull were held in higher esteem than Mr. Scatcherd. He had a large family, three members of which came to Canada; John, Thomas and Lavinia. An older son, James Newton Scatcherd, a commissioned officer in the British army under Sir John Moore, died while on active service in Spain."

Lavinia Scatcherd was the wife of Dr. James Campbell, of Montreal, and mother of the Hon. Alexander Camp-

4

bell, Barrister-at-Law; a Privy Councilor and Life Senator
of the Dominion, who has successively filled, in the government of Canada, the Cabinet offices of Commissioner
of Crown Lands and Postmaster-General; and at present holds ministerial office in the Cabinet as Receiver-
General of Public Revenue.

The pen lingers beside the grave just closed at ancient
Wyton in England, before opening to view the hopeful
adventurous footsteps leading to beautiful young Wyton
of the woodlands in Western Canada. It lingers, held
back by a desire to write more, and still more, of the
amiable Thomas Scatcherd of Hull. But lapse of time,
with remoteness of place, covers in obscurity the uncol-
lected matter of the unwritten record.

CHAPTER II.

JOHN SCATCHERD, popularly Squire Scatcherd of Wyton, father of the subject of this Memoir, was born at Beverley, in Yorkshire, on twenty-first of January, 1800. When nine years of age he was left an orphan. At the age of sixteen he left school and quickly decided on a future career. Familiarity with ships in the Humber, and inspired with songs of the sea, then common to every patriotic boy in England, led this lively lad to engage as a sailor in the Baltic trade. The prospect was a ship of his own to command soon as competent; with several ships and much merchandise to accumulate in the ports of Hull or London when older.

The voyages to St. Petersburg in summer were pleasant; in the latter end of the year, disagreeably otherwise. The ship was driven by storms through blinding snow; the deck and rigging coated with ice, and the salt junk not good. Prolonged passages out and home, with midnight duties often calling him aloft, took all the poetry out of him for " a life on the ocean wave." When Thomas, his brother, filled with a lively desire to wear a

suit of blue and visit foreign countries, ran to meet him
on the wharf, and said: "How do you like being a
sailor?" he was answered, "Tom, I am going to swallow
the mast." That was the figurative expression of sailors
when a shipmate decided, without giving notice, he would
not be on board when his vessel left port.

John Scatcherd, tired of the sea, determined to be a
farmer. In pursuance of that intention, he was articled
for three years to practically learn agriculture with Mr.
Jobson, an extensive farmer near Belford, county of
Northumberland. He left Hull to enter upon this term
of education on Wednesday, thirty-first January, 1817.
The conditions were: Payment of fifty guineas per
annum; and in return to receive board and lodging, with
continuous practice in every department of Northumbrian
farming, at that time, as still, the best system of culture
in England. Mr. Scatcherd now found an occupation
congenial to his taste, and felt a pride and pleasure in
pursuing it. This love for agriculture never throughout
life forsook him. The following letter expresses his satisfaction, and no doubt had much to do in deciding
Thomas to become a farmer also:

NEWTOWN, BELFORD, NORTHUMBERLAND,
May 25, 1817.

Dear Thomas: You must excuse me for not writing
to you sooner, for, really, I have had so much to do I can
scarcely find time to write to any of my friends. I under-

stand you are determined to be a farmer. I will endeavour to give you a particular account of my own situation: In the first place, I get up every morning at half-past four; clean my horses; fodder them; get my breakfast at five o'clock; have my horses harnessed by six, and be ready when the steward calls for the ploughmen. I am always either ploughing or harrowing. We loose at eleven, yoke again at half-past one and quit at six. The horses are foddered at eight, and I generally get in bed between nine and ten o'clock. If you were to come, you would have exactly the same to do for the first year or two, or, perhaps, longer. We have five boys about the size of you and I that do exactly the same work. Besides these boys there are five men. Each has two horses, and nothing else to do but take care of his own. Ploughing is one of the finest jobs you can do; I take very great delight in it. To be a good plougher is one of the principal things in a farmer's business. I can assure you, Thomas, I think farming one of the finest and pleasantest lives a man can lead, and I am extremely fond of it myself. If you are to be a farmer, you could not learn it better than in this county with Mr. Jobson, who, I am sure, would take very great pains in teaching you everything that is necessary to make you a farmer. And let me advise you to make up your mind to something, as you have not long to stay at Cottingham. You must not think you will be a farmer or anything else without considering well what you propose doing.

With best love, I remain, dear Thomas, ever affectionately yours,

JOHN SCATCHERD.

At end of his term of three years, Mr. Scatcherd determined on going to Canada and there purchase land. Such a life as he proposed suited his tastes. His whole ambition was to acquire and possess a goodly number of acres of fertile soil, covered with a natural forest, so that he might clear it with his own hands and have a farm to his liking. On the fourth of April, 1821, he sailed for America in the ship Isabella of Hull, with a fair wind and fine day. He had just passed his twenty-first year.

When arrived at Little York, now Toronto, Mr. Scatcherd was much disappointed at the roughness and rawness of the new country, and thought seriously of returning home. While thus undecided about his next step, he met Colonel Adamson, an old acquaintance and friend of the family, who had come over in the same ship. The colonel expressed himself as perfectly satisfied, and spoke so hopefully and confidently of Canada's prospects and future greatness, that his young friend, concealing his own thoughts and feelings, decided to remain and take his chances in the young colony.

While Mr. Scatcherd was in conversation with Colonel Adamson, a bystander heard him say he was desirous to obtain for a farm a piece of land that had all the trees on it, and where he would have no neighbor near him. The stranger introduced himself, saying he could supply the want, as he had three hundred acres of wild land in the township of Nissouri, with a beautiful trout stream running through it, distant from Little York one hundred and twenty miles west. A bargain was soon effected; a deed, dated thirtieth June, 1821, executed and delivered. Mr. Scatcherd was now owner of the coveted tract of land, with "all the trees on," without having seen it.

The next thing was to find this newly-acquired estate. He was directed to make his way along the lake shore to Hamilton, and then go westward, inquiring for " Bold Kelly," who kept a tavern in Westminster and would furnish directions for the rest of the journey.

Packing a few necessary articles in convenient form, the adventurer set out on foot and alone with his burden on shoulder. After five days of weary toil, making his way through swamps and over treacherous mire holes, wading streams, combating voracious flies, and without meeting one single human being as a traveler on the whole journey, he found himself face to face with the long-desired " Bold Kelly." In the afternoon of the same day he made the acquaintance of a man named Gardener Merrick, living near by, who, chancing to call at Kelly's, invited the new-comer to his home. The hospitable offer was thankfully accepted; and the kind attentions received in that primitive woodland home, was ever afterwards gratefully remembered. Mr. Merrick was a pioneer; a genial and hospitable man. Nature seemed to have made him for a backwoodsman. Forests, swamps,

venomous flies, had no terrors for him.   He had the
happy faculty of impressing on others the charm he felt
in overcoming obstacles and difficulties incidental to life
in a new country.

After resting two days, Mr. Scatcherd made another
start for his new home in the woods.   The directions
were, that he should follow the sled road until it reached
a certain hill; that he should go thence along the hill-
side to the river Thames; up the river bank to the first
small creek; up the creek to the first clearing; and—
"that is the place."

It was early in the morning of a beautiful day in July,
that he set out on this part of the journey of discovery.
After walking fourteen miles in the forest, part of the
distance on a sled road and the balance without a track
up the river and creek, he found himself on the much-
coveted land.   There was on it a rude trough-covered log
hut, an opening in the roof serving for chimney.   On
four acres the timber was cut down; three acres cleared
and planted with turnips, potatoes and buckwheat.

After surveying the premises and building on the outside, he opened the door and walked in.   There were no
locks to doors, nor tramps in those days.   The house was
without rooms.   The roughly-hewed troughs forming the
roof answered equally well for a ceiling.   The floor was
made of split timber, the hearth of dry clay, and the
andirons were small boulders.   Apart from a bedstead,

rigged on split poles, the only piece of furniture was a four-legged bench, made of a slab cut from a tree with an axe. The proprietor sat down to rest with feelings of utter loneliness and desolation. For the first time he fully realized his presence there to be voluntary banishment. Little more than twenty-one years of age, without kindred, friend or acquaintance near him, he was not only a stranger in a strange land, but an inexperienced youth. Accustomed to the social privileges and refinements of city life in the Old World, he was now in the wilderness, solitary, alone.

John Scatcherd, in his solitude, spent the afternoon on the banks of the creek, and in looking over his new purchase. The woods abounded with partridge, wild turkey and deer; the creek with immense quantities of speckled trout. Beneath the trees the land was covered with luxuriant vegetation, waist high. Wherever turning, he saw proofs of a rich and fertile soil. Sunset found him with more hopeful feelings, and with a renewed determination to clear up the farm. The first night spent in his own house was one of intermittent sleep, varied by a sense of loneliness and alarm. Inside legions of mosquitoes paid him their attention. Outside wolves made the forest tremble with their howling. He could hear them breaking the bushes in the near distance, as they changed positions around the small clearing. He expected to find them in the morning waiting for him at the door; but

when daylight came all was peace and solitude once
more. With sunrise buoyancy of spirits returned. After
naming the farm Wyton, and the streamlet River Wye,
the lord of the freehold of Wyton began operations by
the easy task of burning some brush-heaps.

The solitary settler had been told that when desiring
to find his nearest neighbor, he should look for a "blaze"
at one corner of the clearing; and following that about
two miles, he would come to the Bailey settlement. Th
"blaze" was perseveringly sought; but as no signs of
fire or burning could be found, the search was given up.
The instructors had omitted to explain the nature of
those finger-boards of the forest; they were marks made
by an axe on bark of trees to point the way through
pathless woods.

The next day Mr. Scatcherd returned to the house of
Mr. Merrick, and from him obtained two axes, provisions,
and much valuable information, the nature of which he
was beginning to understand and appreciate. At the
Merrick homestead he met a man known as Doctor Newland, who wished employment. An engagement was
made and the two started for Wyton, each carrying an
axe in hand and a load of provisions on shoulder. They
took a nearer route home, the Doctor, an experienced
woodsman, leading. He boasted of ability to find his
way through the densest forest by day or night. Why
he was called Doctor was then a mystery to the oldest

inhabitant, and so, doubtless, will remain. He was an American; wore buckskin knee-breeches, and had his hair tied into a queue, vulgarly a pigtail. This appendage he regarded with excessive tenderness. The Doctor's best known accomplishment was that of cook. In this capacity his rare ability found full scope.

The first dinner being over, and the Doctor washing the dishes, his employer thought he would try the new axe cutting down his first tree. He selected a cherry stub, dry as a bone, thinking it would cut easy because it had no limbs. They who understand the different kinds of wood in Canada, know he had chosen one of the worst trees for his purpose; in such a condition it was scarcely less hard than lignum-vitæ. The afternoon was nearly over, and his hands covered with blisters, before the cherry stub fell. When that time came, Mr. Scatcherd understood how arduous is the labor of clearing a farm, especially to one not brought up as a backwoodsman, and, as it were, "to the manor born." All thought of clearing away the forest with his own hands was abandoned. The stump of the cherry tree remained until the year 1848. It stood in the field now inclosed by pine trees of his own planting, and was often pointed to as showing how much or how little he had known about chopping. Other men were now hired, and fields cleared, fenced and planted.

During the summer of 1822, Mr. Scatcherd was joined
by his brother Thomas. They had a happy meeting.
Thomas brought a large budget of news, of which the
comparatively old settler was anxious to learn every item.
The only difficulty was to find time to tell and to listen.

On the first of August, 1822, Mr. John Scatcherd was
married to Miss Anne Farley, who was born in the county
of Armagh, Ireland, in the year 1802. She was daughter
of Mr. John Farley, of whom more is related presently.

For the sake of contrasting the present with the past,
and to benefit those contemplating weddings and wed-
ding trips, it may not be uninteresting to state how the
day of the marriage was spent. Throughout the morning the groom was diligently employed thatching a hay-
stack. After dinner he made his toilet, and taking on his
shoulder part of a sack of flour, with which to repay a
loan of the same kind, and carrying the wedding-coat on
his arm, he set out for the residence of the bride, nearly
two miles distant. At four o'clock in the afternoon the
ceremony was performed by Charles Ingersoll, Esquire,
J. P., then an active magistrate, residing in the county of
Oxford, where the town of Ingersoll now stands, brother
of Mr. James Ingersoll, present Registrar of that county.
Magistrates in those days officiated when clergymen were
not residing within eighteen miles of the residence of
bride or groom. In such cases the law required an ad-
vertisement to be posted at the crossing of roads or other

places available for publicity. This public notice was posted :

WHEREAS, John Scatcherd and Anne Farley, both of the township of Nissouri, are desirous of intermarrying with each other, and there being no parson or minister of the Church of England living within eighteen miles of them, or either of them, all persons who know any just cause or impediment why they should not be joined together in matrimony, are requested to give notice thereof to Charles Ingersoll, one of His Majesty's Justices of the Peace for the District of London.

CHARLES INGERSOLL.

OXFORD, *10th July, 1822.*

Soon as the marriage knot was tied, the newly-married couple set out for their future home. On arriving there the first duties of the young bride were performed in preparing their evening meal.

CHAPTER III.

THOMAS SCATCHERD, the newly-arrived brother, was born in Hull, on thirtieth April, 1802. In his fifteenth year, he decided to learn the art of agriculture and live the life of a farmer. With that object in view he, in the month of December, 1817, left school and was articled to a farmer in Northumberland, near Belford, in the same locality where his brother John was then indentured. The articles bound Thomas for a term of four years; and, in addition to his personal services, he paid a premium of fifty guineas annually.

The harvests of 1816 and 1817 were deplorably late, and all grain crops of poor quality. In Northumberland, as elsewhere on the English and Scottish borders in 1817, much of the oat crop, and most of the peas and beans, were carried in the straw to be trampled by cattle for manure. The meal for human food was made from grain, maltened in the sheaves. During that dreary winter, when the youthful apprentice to agriculture was eating scones made from the meal of bad barley and unripe beans, helping in the threshing-mill to dress moldy

wheat for market, he became discouraged and wished to
go again to school. But the genial summer of 1818
brought to him better health and greater strength; and
to the country an abundant harvest. Letters of affectionate solicitude came from the family home. One from
Emily, added to the outflow of a sister's love the cheer-
ing suggestion that he might, in the future, live near
them as a Yorkshire farmer. The Cheviot Hills looked
less gloomy; Chillingham Park, with its herds of aborig-
inal wild cattle, became beautiful. All nature was radi-
ant, glad and fruitful. With sunshine in his soul the
city-bred boy felt a new joy, a new hope, and decided to
be a master in the art of agriculture.

Extract from Emily's Letter.

NEWLAND, BEVERLEY, *February 4, 1818.*

My Dearest Brother : I often think if you get to be
a clever farmer, Lord Fitzwilliam, who was one of your
father's most intimate friends, will let you a farm of his,
if you do not purchase one of your own. He is an excellent and good man. How delighted we would all be to
have you near us, a successful Yorkshire farmer.

After the first year's experience, Thomas became ardently attached to agricultural life, and continued satisfied
with the choice he had made. Before his indenture expired, although well advised by John of the difficulties
and hardships incident to clearing up a farm in the woods,

he resolved to join his brother in America, and with him share his lot in life. In the spring of 1822, after completing what he considered a proper outfit, the young farmer took passage for Canada in the good ship Isabella of Hull. Arriving safely at Quebec, he proceeded by steamer to Montreal. This vessel catching fire he nearly lost his outfit, but succeeded in saving it, although in a much-damaged condition. From Montreal his journey was by wagon to Lachine; thence to Prescott by bateau. Taking a schooner there he sailed for Hamilton, landing at Chisholm's wharf on a Saturday, putting up at Chisholm's tavern and remaining there over Sunday. Landing his goods, he hired two teams to take him and the outfit to Bold Kelly's, a distance of some seventy miles. For this service he paid twenty-four dollars. After resting a night he set out, with Bold Kelly as guide, to find his brother. They had one horse between them, and each walked and rode alternately. Arriving at Wyton on eighteenth of June, 1822, and finding no one in the house, they went to the field and found his brother and Doctor Newland hoeing corn, which was then six inches high. After fraternal greetings the news followed; but with much to tell on one side, inquire about and listen to on the other, the economical use of time suggested itself. John handed to his brother a hoe, saying, " We will work and talk too." Thomas took the implement and vigorously applied it around stumps and among roots, making sad havoc with the young pumpkin plants, not knowing them from nettles and other weeds. So passed the first afternoon.

The second day was devoted to calling on some of the neighbors. The first call made was on Mr. John Farley, who had settled a year or two earlier; and who, besides being one of the oldest settlers, had an interesting family—two of them young ladies. Between the eldest and John a friendship, mutually agreeable, had already been formed. The remainder of that day was spent in making calls on neighbors in the Bailey settlement. Night found Thomas tired and exhausted, principally from efforts in walking along small poles, which formed the bridges over streams and swamps, one pole making a bridge. Thick-soled shoes with hobnails and iron-shod heels, rendered the crossing of those bridges peculiarly difficult and tiresome.

The neighbors called on informed their neighbors of the arrival of the young Englishman, and, in turn, showed their respect and gratified curiosity by visiting him and his brother. The first introduction was: " Thomas, I make you acquainted with Uncle Perkins." The next was: " Thomas, I make you acquainted with Father Comstock." The third was: " Thomas, I make you acquainted with my friend George Belton." Then: " Thomas, I make you acquainted with neighbor Thomas Howay." To all of whom Thomas expressed his pleas-

5

ure in making their acquaintance with a bow, the essence of politeness and respect. As information of the newly-arrived settler spread wider and wider, new and hitherto unheard-of Fathers and Uncles made their calls; many of them barefooted and some bareheaded. The idea of finding so many Fathers and Uncles in the wilderness was as agreeable as it was puzzling.

In due time the two wagon-loads of outfit left at Bold Kelly's were brought home. The preparation made in England, for the journey and new country to which Thomas was going, indicated, in part, his estimate of what might be required. Along with many, very many, other things, useful and useless, was an assortment of tools, including everything from gimlets to augers, and chisels to axes. Some of the axes were sixteen inches long from the edge to the eye; ship-carpenters' axes, utterly unfit for a farmer's use, either in hewing or chopping. Next followed grain measures; bushels, half-bushels, pecks and half-pecks; each handled, bound, and strapped with hoop-iron. An assortment of buttons so large that the supply has not been exhausted in the intervening fifty-six years. Corkscrews in such abundance, they also have lasted to the present time.

In those days such articles held a prominent place; nothing could go well, or pass off friendly and smoothly, unless there was something comforting around, requiring the services of a corkscrew. A medicine-chest, parti-

tioned off into numerous divisions, contained vials—
round, square and octagon—of all dimensions; their
labels covering nearly all the known remedies for disease
or accident. The medicine-chest was supplemented by a
canteen done off into larger compartments, filled with
medicine in bulk. Those two articles are yet on duty,
and, unless destroyed by fire or flood, are likely to last
for generations to come; nothing short of axe or sledge
could damage them. The strength with which they
were constructed indicates the hardships they were
expected to endure before reaching their destination.
Two guns, four pistols, and ammunition by the hundred-
weight. A bale of mosquito netting. An ample ward-
robe, in which hose led all other articles in quantity.
Shirt collars, whose ample spread when in position
reached the ears. A full dress suit of blue broadcloth
with brass buttons, the collar of the swallow-tailed coat
reaching half-way up the head. A black hat, very
high, bell-crowned and narrow-brimmed. It would be
rank injustice not to mention an overcoat, called Fear-
naught. It was drab-colored, immensely high-collared,
had three capes, broad belt, huge buttons, and when
worn touched the feet. To the extent of ownership
only, could this coat be considered individual property.
For over fifty winters it served the owner and his family,
besides doing constant duty in the settlement; no long
journey would be undertaken without knowing whether

"Uncle Tom's" great-coat might be counted on or not.
Once within its generous folds, with all the large buttons
fastened, pelting storms or biting frosts were powerless
to harm. It also served as bed-quilt and horse cover,
and still survives the wear and tear of time. During
the spring of 1878 it was put on for exhibition, but
minus capes and belt. If true merit were a guarantee
against oblivion, this coat would long be remembered.
Surely no coat ever better deserved the name of GREAT-
coat, than this good old servant did.

Thomas had just passed his twentieth year, was slender
and delicate in physique, and when attired in his elegant
full dress suit, including high hat and bright bandanna,
was certainly out of all proper keeping and character
with his surroundings. A position in a counting-house,
or as a private secretary, might have seemed in accordance with the fitness of things; but the idea of a youth
of his age, and apparently delicate strength, undertaking
to meet and overcome the hardships and struggles incident to clearing up and making a farm in the wilderness, seemed preposterous in the extreme. His appearance did not reflect his thoughts or feelings. He had
spent considerable time and means in learning the art of
farming. He had come a long distance to put it in
practice. He was prepared to encounter hardships,
struggle with difficulties, and bound to overcome them.
His greatest desire was to make a beginning; but think-

ing it better not to be too hasty in purchasing land, he concluded to remain awhile with his brother and gain some practical knowledge of the country. Not being robust, he undertook to perform the duties of the culinary department.

The Doctor, who had hitherto done the cooking, was now relieved. The new cook succeeded to the entire satisfaction of all concerned but himself. His disappointment and dissatisfaction arose from the ever-continuing difficulty of keeping his dish-towels clean. Soak, boil and pound them as he might, still the grease and rusty color remained. To replace them with new ones was a serious matter, when a yard of cotton or coarse linen was worth two bushels of wheat. Relating his distress and trouble one day to friend George Belton (who had mastered the art) he was told to put ashes in the water when he boiled his towels. The advice was followed with a result far beyond expectation. After rinsing the towels their whiteness and cleanness surprised and delighted him. It is doubtful if any improvement he found in after-life pleased him as much.

In 1823 Thomas purchased four hundred acres of land adjacent to his brother's estate and began clearing it. The difficulty of crossing pole bridges did not prevent frequent visits to Mr. Farley's. The explanation of those visits might have been found in the person of a graceful young lady who had just said good-bye to sweet sixteen.

The visits increased in number and grew in interest until, on the fifth day of February, 1824, Thomas Scatcherd and Miss Jane Farley were made one. The young couple at once began housekeeping in their own home, and together shared each other's burdens and toils. They had a numerous family, seventeen in all; five dying in their infancy, the others growing up to man and woman-hood.

As year by year passed, the forests on the lot disappeared, and field after field was added to the farm. A resolution and energy, backed with a perseverance that knew nothing of failure, succeeded in converting one of the heaviest timbered lots in the county into a farm at once beautiful and prolific. Shortly after marriage the young couple showed their good sense by uniting with a church. Both were members of the Established Church of England; but as there were no services of that communion in the neighborhood, they united with the Methodists, and lived God-fearing lives; an honor to the Church, and an example to others worthy of imitation.

On the twentieth day of November, 1865, death darkened and desolated that happy home, removing from it the beloved wife and affectionate mother. For over forty-one years she had devotedly lived and toiled for her family. The cares and anxieties of this mother's heart none can tell but He who knoweth all things. The proper care and training of a family so large in a newly-settled country calls for a love and devotion that forgets self and surrenders all but a mother's love.

Mr. Scatcherd, in his seventy-seventh year, is still living on the old homestead, enjoying the reward of his early toils and struggles. Although not robust in health, few men have the good fortune to arrive at his years in possession of faculties and strength so little impaired. The evening hours of his life are soothed and cheered by the filial love and unremitting attention of his youngest daughter Lavinia. Were it possible to repay the debt of love and gratitude due a parent, this daughter's indebtedness might be considered canceled.

In politics Mr. Scatcherd may be said to have been born a Reformer. Through life he has voted as a Reformer, and will die a Reformer. In the election of 1878 he went to the poll and voted with all the glow of younger days. In looking over the past he considers that the early years in his log-house were the happiest, though toil was hardest. "Politics," says Uncle Thomas, "had not then stirred up strife between neighbors. Nor was selfishness so apparent as now. Mutual dependence was followed by mutual assistance. This fraternity of wants and sympathies bound us together. All were glad to know of the well-doing and well-being of one another."

CHAPTER IV.

Mr. John Farley.

M R. JOHN FARLEY, father-in-law of Messrs. John and Thomas Scatcherd, was born in Armagh, Ireland. Leaving his native country for America with his wife and four children, Anne, James, Jane and Turner, aged respectively eighteen, sixteen, fourteen and ten years, he arrived in Little York, now Toronto, June 22, 1820. From there he moved into the township of Nissouri, on Lot Seven, Second Concession; arriving on the future farm during the latter part of September of the same year. Roads were so bad, the last nine miles, they had to complete the journey on foot, carrying on their backs provisions and such articles of household necessity as could not be dispensed with.

There were no improvements on the lot; not a stick had been cut. Shelter for the family must be provided. Taking advantage of a turned up root, leaning poles against it and covering them with brush, a home in the woods was secured until a small log-house covered with split white-ash staves was put up, and considered a luxury, although without chimney or ceiling. During the

winter, sufficient skill in handling the axe was acquired
to chop three acres of forest, which was cleared in the
early spring without the help of oxen. When ready for
the seed, two bushels and one peck of wheat was all the
grain that could be found for love or money. After
much deliberation, one bushel of wheat was sowed on
the first acre; three pecks on the second acre; and two
pecks on the third acre. By exchanging work with a
neighbor, a yoke of oxen was secured to harrow in the
wheat.

The harrow, or drag as commonly called, was **V**-
shaped, made from the fork of a tree, with wooden pins
inserted for teeth. Persons not acquainted with the
roughness of a new piece of ground when first cleared,
can form no idea of undertaking to harrow in seed with
a drag having wooden teeth; but those familiar with
this kind of work, will appreciate the difficulty and
wonder how anything short of a factory could keep a
drag supplied with wooden pegs until three acres of
wheat were well covered on new land. Although the proportion of seed sown on each acre was so unequal, the
difference in the yield of grain was not discernible. During the ensuing winter a yoke of oxen, a cow and nine
real iron harrow teeth were added to the farm; the teeth
being each twelve inches long and an inch and a half
square. When the teeth were in position, in a drag made

of oak timber six by eight inches square, it was' a formidable agricultural implement.

Mr. Farley was unfortunate while chopping, toward the latter part of the winter 1822, in cutting one of his legs very badly. Before the blood could be stopped he nearly bled to death. Although able to assist a little in planting and harvesting, he never fully recovered from the effects of losing so much blood. On nineteenth of August, 1822, the first sad wave of affliction and sorrow broke over the young settlement. Mr. Farley, feeling unable to continue his work in the harvest field, came home early in the afternoon complaining he did not feel well. By midnight he was so much worse Doctor Duncombe of Burford, forty miles' distant, was sent for. Meanwhile everything that family and neighbors could do was done. Still each hour that passed left him worse. On the third day of this aggravated sickness he died. The disease was intermittent fever of a malignant type. As the doctor could be of no benefit now, a messenger was sent to meet him and announce the death of the patient. This death brought sadness and darkness to relatives and neighbors alike. John Farley was the idol and favorite of the settlement.

A sad duty after death is the necessity of making preparations for returning the dearest object of the affections to the dust. The mournful office on this occasion was intensified by the difficulty of procuring materials necessary for burial purposes. Linen sheets by aching hearts were converted into habiliments for the coffin. But where was the coffin to come from, when there was no undertaker to furnish it, nor material to make it of? While the necessity of digging out the trunk of a tree for a coffin seemed the only expedient, the perplexity was settled by the arrival of a yoke of oxen, sled and driver. The oxen, with heads high, moved actively as horses; the tips of their long spreading horns, jet black, glistened as if polished. They were owned and driven by Mr. George Belton. This gentleman resided a little over two miles distant, on First Lot, Second Concession, Township of London. Soon as Mr. Belton heard of the death of his neighbor, the difficulty of procuring a coffin suggested itself. Having at considerable trouble secured two boards for a special purpose, he concluded to take them and see if they were required. Yoking his oxen to a sled, he put on the boards and brought them along; thus greatly relieving his heart-broken friends. Viewed from the stand-point of value, the kindness amounted to but little; estimated by the want supplied, it was immeasurable; and as such was received and remembered. Although the very best the neighbors could do, the coffin when finished was a rough piece of workmanship.

At the funeral all the men, women and children of the settlement were present; some coming on ox-sleds

and others on foot. No clergyman being available, the
funeral services consisted of singing a hymn, in which all
joined, and by Mr. Robert Webster reading a prayer.
The number at the funeral was not large, but the sympathy was heartfelt and genuine. Every step taken on way
to the burial-place was a step of sadness and solemnity.
And when the coffin was lowering into the grave it
seemed as if all earthly hopes were disappearing. There
being no burying-ground, the deceased was interred on
his own farm. Twenty-four years later, his remains were
transferred to Robin's Hill, where they now repose alongside those of his beloved wife, who died in October,
1846.

The duty of managing and clearing up the farm now
fell upon the two boys, and never did sons more willingly
meet and do their duty. Land was cleared and fenced;
a house and barn built; horses, cows and sheep added to
the farm.

James, having a taste for business, went into London,
formed a partnership with a Mr. Jones of London township, and carried on a general store. He married Miss
Jones, daughter of his partner. She died in 1836, leaving three children. Not being successful in business, he
articled himself as a student-at-law with his nephew, the
late Thomas Scatcherd, and remained in his office until
expiration of the articles. Shortly after being admitted
attorney-at-law, Mr. Farley received the appointment of

Clerk of the Peace for the county of Elgin, and moved to St. Thomas. The office was held until his death. Surviving all his children, he died on twenty-sixth of March, 1875.

The youngest son, Turner, a justice of the peace, is still on the homestead, hale and strong; and at his ease and leisure enjoying the fruits of his early hardships and struggles. In 1833 he married Miss Georgiana Phillips, of Freligsburg, Lower Canada, a young lady of superior education, who shared the toils and labors of her husband, and with him is now enjoying the fruits of their united industry. They raised a family of six children. The eldest, John, is a successful barrister in St. Thomas, having a large practice, and to the fullest extent enjoying the confidence and esteem of his fellow-townsmen. The youngest, James, a graduate of McGill College, Montreal, is practicing medicine in the United States.

CHAPTER V.

The Lost Neighbors.

DURING the spring of 1822 an event took place which drew out the sympathies of the young settlement to their utmost tension. Although the incident may have but little direct connection with the subject of this volume it is included to give an idea of the extent of the wilderness in which John Scatcherd and his brother had settled.

Thomas Howay had settled on a lot of land in the township of London, a little over one mile distant from Wyton, the Thames running through the lot. One morning while at work he heard an unusual noise across the river, and on going to the nearest point of view saw some men, with guns and dogs, greatly excited. They had followed three bears to the river. The bears took to the water and swam across; but the stream being too deep to ford, with no other means for getting over, the hunters could not follow. Howay, excited and eager for the chase, ran to Wyton and informed Dr. Newland, who, according to his own estimate, was one of the greatest bear hunters in the country. "If," he used to say, "I am good for anything at all it is for killing bar."

It was not long until Howay and the Doctor, with their guns and dogs, were in hot pursuit. A light fall of snow during the early morning greatly facilitated following the bears. The hunters were fresh and eager, the dogs fierce and keen. The bears, finding themselves closely pressed, took refuge in a monster water elm, in the Doctor's language, "tall as a pine and straight as an arrow." This tree stood on Lot Nine, Third Concession of West Nissouri. The farm is now owned by Mr. J. Henderson. It is but a few years since the remains of this elm were piled together at a logging-bee, and burned.

High in the tree top the bears concealed themselves in a large hollow completely out of sight. The noise made by the hunters and dogs induced one of the bears to put his head out and take a view of matters below. Quick as thought the trusty old smooth-bore flashed. The bear gave a terrific roar, sprang from its den, plunging and crashing down through the limbs and branches of the trees beneath. The hunters felt they had reached a point where it was either life or death, and prepared for a hand-to-hand conflict with an enraged and wounded bear. Great was their relief on realizing that the unerring aim of Howay had proved fatal to bruin. The bear was doubtless dead before it reached the ground, the bullet having entered at under part of the neck, and passed out at base of the brain. The hunters being so much elated and excited over this success, determined to have the other bears. Howay having killed one felt like killing another; and the Doctor, feeling his laurels somewhat shorn, was ambitious to redeem himself. One of them went for re-enforcements and axes, while the other, with the dogs, kept guard at base of the tree. On arrival of the recruits, axes, wielded by brawny arms strong and willing, filled the air with chips, many of them popping like pistols as they started from the kerf; while the best shots prepared their guns and selected the most available positions for execution. The afternoon was well nigh gone before the wavering top of the huge tree gave indication of the coming crash. The excitement of men and dogs was intense. A few more well-directed blows, and down starts the sturdy elm, carrying with it a small forest of branches, limbs and smaller trees. The bears did not show themselves until just before their falling den touched the ground; and then, as the hunters were ranged on opposite sides, fear of shooting each other prevented a free use of their guns. Between the confusion and the excitement the bears, partly protected by the limbs and brush, made good their escape, one un- harmed, the other slightly wounded. Then began a chase in earnest; the pursuers intending to tree the bears again, and the bears, doubtless profiting by their recent experience, determined to trust no more in the uncer- tainty of trees.

One by one the pursuers fell to the rear and returned home, until only the Doctor and Howay were left; having with them an axe, gun and dog. They followed the tracks until nightfall, and then by starlight until completely tired out. Coming across a hollow tree they slept in it over night, and considered they had comfortable quarters. In the morning they shot a partridge, and roasting it for breakfast started afresh after the bears. During the day a shower of rain took away the snow, which prevented them from longer following the tracks. They very reluctantly gave up the chase; then hungry and tired turned for home. Not reaching home by dark they built a fire, made the most of it during the night, starting early next morning to complete their journey. Without any food they traveled all day. The distance seemed never-ending. The Doctor, on account of his boasted skill in the woods had led the way, feeling confident he was right. He accounted for the long distance required to reach home by insisting that while they were fresh and under the excitement of the chase, they had traveled many miles farther than supposed. Seeing a light curl of smoke in the distance they concluded they must be near the settlement, and that the weary hours of hunger and tramping would soon be over. On approaching the fire they were horrified and amazed at finding themselves on the identical spot where they had spent the previous night. Their hearts sank

6   -

within them. They knew they had described the inevi-
table circle of the lost and bewildered.

The sky was cloudy and heavy. The weather had
turned cold and they were chilled through, hungry and
weary. But although much alarmed, both felt confident
they would be able to find a way out to the clearing the
coming day. The night was spent in keeping up their
fire, deploring their condition, making plans for the next
day, and sleeping but very little. Starting in the morning
they laid their course with all the care and skill they were
masters of; carefully observed the moss on the trees;
fixed their attention on objects in the distance, and
walked direct to them. They moved slowly and cau-
tiously, using all the precaution woodmen take for their
guidance. The forenoon and afternoon seemed flying as
never so quickly before. Evening was soon followed by
inky darkness. The day's work had to be given up,
they as much in the wilderness as yesterday. They had
satisfied their hunger with buds, roots, and the bark of
slippery-elm trees. Another restless, shivering night was
passed; and to add to their misfortune the days and
nights were still cold and cloudy; and being without a
compass they had nothing but the moss on the trees to
guide them. The fifth day was the first one really unsat-
isfactory. It was largely spent in disputing and disagree-
ing as to which was the right or the wrong course to
take. Sometimes one would insist on being the leader,

and after hours of protests and fault-finding on the part of the other, would give up, saying: "Now you try it, and see if you can do better."

Leaving the hunters awhile, we find at home there was anxiety and fears. The non-return of the men the first day excited no surprise, as remaining over one night in the woods was a common occurrence; but seeing nothing of them on the second day was alarming. The third morning a few of the neighbors set out and spent the day in searching the woods; and seeing or hearing nothing of them, came to the conviction they were lost. The alarm being spread far and wide, every neighbor telling his neighbor, the whole country was soon out on the search. Horns were blown, guns fired, and fires built at night, but no success. A fruitless week was spent without a clue to the lost settlers. Thirty miles distant had been heard from, but no intelligence of the Doctor, Howay, or the dog. Most reluctantly the search was given up, the conclusion being arrived at that the Doctor and Howay were hopelessly lost, or had been devoured by wild beasts. Mr. Scatcherd and his brother offered a reward to any who might find them; after which the people settled down to their usual every-day life again.

Returning to the hunters, we find the sixth day was but little different from the fifth, except that confidence in each other began to diminish. The anxiety, along with cold, hunger and fatigue, made them irritable in the

extreme. The dog made night hideous, howling for
want of food; while its masters were afraid to go to
sleep lest one might in desperation take some advantage
of the other. In the early part of this day their mutual
distrust led to separation. Taking opposite directions
they were soon out of sight of each other, without wishing or expecting to meet again. In this they were disappointed. As the darkness of night was settling down
they met not far from the place of parting. This meeting was dismally bewildering; and a proof that they
were helplessly and hopelessly lost. Worse than lost,
unable to get away from each other. They spent the
night without fire, and scarcely exchanged words. The
seventh day they wandered aimlessly around, sullen and
gloomy; hunger pinching and irritating them; and all
the while their suspicions of one another increasing.
Each often eyed the dog and thought how good it would
taste; but neither dared express his thoughts, fearing
the horrible suggestion it might beget.

The eighth day one of them refused to walk ahead;
and, being the stronger, insisted upon and made the other
walk before him. In the afternoon they came to a large
stream. This revived their courage and spirits; and, to
some extent, renewed good feeling towards each other.
They determined to follow the river downward, believing
it must bring them out at some place if their strength
permitted them to follow it. A little after sundown they

came to where some one had cut and stacked wild grass. They took up their quarters under shelter of the friendly hay-stack, and passed the night with dreams of coming relief, partially forgetting sufferings and fears.

Next morning before it was fairly daylight, they started down the river and made good progress, until they came to where a large swamp emptied into the stream. Not being able to get over, they undertook to go around it. On and on they struggled and still there was no end to the swamp, nor opportunity to cross it. Coming to what appeared to be a large bend or curve, they concluded to save time and distance by going straight across. After eating some roots and bark, and resting a little, they started again, keeping the swamp as they supposed just in sight. Late in the afternoon they were greatly encouraged and cheered in seeing evidence of a clearing ahead of them. This roused their flagging spirits and quickened their steps. On arriving at the supposed clearing they became speechless. They had returned to the hay-stack! Dumb as mutes, stiffened and benumbed, they passed a long and dreary night.

In the morning they separated, to dig and eat roots alone. Howay went to the Doctor and was the first to break silence, by proposing to try and cross the river and get down on the other side. The Doctor fell in with the idea, and both started for a pile of drift-wood they had noticed on their journey down the bank. With much difficulty they succeeded in crossing. On reaching the high land on that side of the stream, they saw an opening in the woods which indicated a clearing. Drawing nearer to it and seeing a small log-house, their hearts bounded with gladness. They became delirious with the joyful excitement, feeling as though they hardly pressed the ground they walked upon. On arriving at the house they found it desolate and deserted, with weeds and briars growing inside. No doubt a discouraged settler, unable to continue his struggles in the wilderness, had been compelled to abandon his little beginning. The disappointment and depression of spirits felt by the hunters were beyond description. They ceased to chide or mistrust each other, and lost all desire to make further efforts to save themselves by continuing their struggles.

While there was nothing to gain by remaining at a deserted house, yet there appeared to be a something connected with it that held them there. Night came on and they, hungry, weary and heart-broken, took shelter beneath the cold and cheerless roof. The fact that it was the only evidence of the existence of human beings they had seen since their wanderings and sufferings commenced, shed a soothing ray of warmth in their sad and weary hearts. The dog, unable to follow them further, was dying at the hay-stack. During the night they heard a cow-bell, and oh! the sweetness of its music. They could not sleep; they sat up and talked and cried with joy. The night seemed endless in its length; daylight would never, never come. They knew if they could reach the cows and start them they would go directly home. Before day had fairly dawned they were up and off for the cattle, falling over logs, stumbling over roots, and tripping at every twig. They did not reach them until nearly noon. The cows becoming frightened started for home direct, leaving their tracks to guide the wanderers.

It was not far from sundown when the two walking skeletons entered a log-house, and frightened the good farmer's wife with their emaciated and worn appearance; their clothes nearly torn off them. It did not take long to explain matters; weakness and starved looks indicated their wants better than words. The Doctor, knowing food in large quantities might prove fatal, requested the farmer and his wife on no account to let them have more than a small quantity at a time, until their stomachs got accustomed to it again. Food was given very sparingly, but disposed of eagerly. The first two days it was necessary to restrain them from eating, they could not control themselves. After restrictions were removed the justice they did to provisions was truly surprising. Next morning the farmer went to the hay-stack and found the dog so weak it could not stand. He carried it in his arms to the house. The kindness of Mr. and Mrs. Townsend was never forgotten by the hunters.

The friendly river proved to be the Sable, which empties
into Lake Huron. During the ten days in the woods,
the men had wandered to a point over thirty miles distant in a direct line from Wyton. Thirty miles of dense
wilderness then, without even a cow-path or Indian trail;
now a beautiful, cleared up country, thickly settled and
in a state of high cultivation.

Soon as strength was acquired to warrant the venture,
the hunters and dog set out for home. Arriving there
they were hardly recognizable; being still so emaciated
and worn, as to be but little other than remnants of their
former selves. Their appearance astounded the community; it was as if they had risen from the dead. Although
they had not been forgotten, all expectation of meeting
them again in the flesh had been given up; and the
only unsolved mystery connected with them was,
whether they had perished from exposure and hunger,
or had fallen a prey to the wolves and bears then so
numerous. It was something remarkable, and often
noticed, that neither the Doctor nor Howay cared for
telling the story of this adventure. They would not
recur to it unless specially urged, and in relating it they
never precisely agreed. Certain parts of the story, each
preferred telling in his own way, and so told it.

Mr. Thomas Scatcherd was at the cutting of the tree
in which the bears took refuge. Having just purchased
a rifle he was anxious to prove its qualities; but for

reasons before given dared not fire, and so lost the opportunity. He is now the sole surviving witness of the fall of the tree and return of the lost neighbors.

Thomas Howay was a generous-hearted Irishman, who settled on Lot One, Fourth Concession of London. His first house was a cave excavated in the side of a hill. While it lacked ventilation and light, it had the advantage of being warm in winter and cool in summer. His physical constitution, like his courage, was robust. With clothes carried on shoulder, he often crossed the river when the water, waist high, was covered with slush-ice. He was a successful farmer and a respected citizen. Thomas Howay died about ten years ago.

Barnadine Newland remained a year or two at Wyton, after the adventure with the bears, and then left to visit his friends. He was not heard of, except by letter, until the year 1872. Then, in old age, the bear-hunting Doctor returned to take a last view of Wyton. He was disappointed. Improvements made in the intervening forty years had transformed the wilderness to farms and fields, fruitful orchards and gardens. The Wye and sloping hill-sides were the only familiar objects remaining. He talked of early times, and inquired about old acquaintances; but said nothing about hunting the bears, until urged to repeat the story, which was done with reluctance and without comment. Dr. Barnadine Newland died in 1873.

CHAPTER VI.

ON the tenth of November, 1823, the first child of John and Anne Scatcherd was born, and named Thomas. The mother requiring breast-glasses, none could be had nearer than Toronto, one hundred and twenty miles distant, over roads which now would be considered almost impassable. Thomas, the brother, started on foot to procure them. The time to go and return was so long they were not required when he arrived home. The adventures of this trip have oft been related by Uncle Tom. In those days the nearest physician was Doctor Duncombe, who lived forty miles away on Burford Plains. It usually required three full days to get the Doctor to the bedside of the patient. It was regarded as almost a rule that if the patient were alive on the arrival of the Doctor, the case would not prove fatal.

In the same early time, two days were required to go to mill and return. Horses and wagons were then not in use; the roads being simply tracks for ox-sleds. They wound about through the woods in zigzag form, avoiding trees, wind-falls, mud-holes and swampy places. They were unfit for any vehicle except a sled drawn by a yoke

of oxen. Six bushels of wheat made a large load, and
two miles an hour fast time. The standard price of a
yard of unbleached cotton was two bushels of wheat.
One pound of tea, three bushels of wheat. One barrel
of salt, ten bushels of wheat. The postage of a letter
from England, three shillings and eight pence sterling—
ninety-two cents.

Church-going was impossible, there being neither
churches nor clergymen in that neighborhood.

The monotony of life in the forest was relieved at
times by letters from loving sisters left in England. Miss
Mary Scatcherd, with charming vivacity, wrote of her
journeys through France, of her residence in Paris, and
of eminent people met in the family circle of the Reverend Mr. Forster, Chaplain to the English Ambassador.
The poet, Thomas Moore, and wife, were of the number.
In 1804, Moore had been in Canada, and, doubtless,
talked with Miss Scatcherd of the woodlands he trav-
ersed from Niagara to Ancaster, Little York and Montreal, and may have sung:

> " I knew by the smoke that so gracefully curled
> Above the green elms, that a cottage was near."

The song of the "Woodpecker," took being and wing at a
lone woodland hut, about two miles north of the present-
day railway station of Bronte, on Toronto Branch of the
Canada Great Western. And at Ste. Anne's, three hun-

dred and fifty miles farther east, a glow of thought and
musical harmony gave birth to the "Canadian Boat-
man's Song." It can hardly be supposed that Miss Mary
did not speak of her dear brothers in Canada, when
Moore sang and told of his travels. Whether so or not,
the following letter, in which Paris is described, came to
her brothers in their far western woodlands, the welcome
communion of a sweet sister.

NEWLAND, *March 16, 1823.*

My Dear Brothers : I have so much to say to you, I
scarcely can tell how to begin.

It is now one year and three months since I left England. I am once again seated quietly at Newland. My
coming home has been much earlier than I at first intended ; but my dear sister Emily so earnestly requested
me to come that I could no longer resist.

When I arrived at Calais, the rapid change of everything about me made me laugh most ridiculously. I had
been but three hours crossing the channel and found
men and women, houses and streets, all so different, it
appeared like the realization of a dream.

I had met with a large party of young people going to
school at Paris, so joined them ; and we all (twenty-three)
set off in a lumbering old vehicle, like a covered gig with
two coaches fastened close behind it, and all our luggage
piled upon the top. This is called a diligence, and is
drawn by four, sometimes six, and even nine horses, harnessed with ropes and going three and four abreast. A
postillion rides one of the shaft horses, and with long

ropes guides the others before him, making such a tre-
mendous noise with his whip, that really it quite frightens
one. Figure to yourself a man dressed in an old sky-
blue jacket, trimmed with tarnished silver, a pair of filthy
nankeens, all shoved up from his legs, which, without any
stockings, and with a pair of clumsy shoes, were thrust
into two great boots, fastened to each side of the saddle,
and which are large enough for a child to stand in. His
powdered hair was tied in a thick club-knot, and by its
motion had thoroughly larded the back of his coat with
grease and powder. Upon his head, a little scrimpy-
looking hat, stuck on one side with a green ribband round
it, and a full-blown rose in front; the hair well frizzed
out under it on each side. This is the common dress of
the country postillions here. In Paris they imitate the
English.

On our way we passed through several fine towns; but
the road is very uninteresting, there is so little wood.
The animals all seemed to me so thin and tall. A sheep
appeared like a dog dressed up, and pigs have such long
legs they look quite graceful.

When arrived in Paris, I could not raise my head from
pain and extreme fatigue, and for several weeks was
scarcely able to crawl about. I went as a boarder in the
school kept by a lady who was teacher where our sister
Emily received her education. This lady's name was Mrs.
Bray. I soon found it was not a place for me, for although
I did as I pleased in many things, there were others very
unpleasant. I endured many discomforts for two months.
At the end of that time Mr. and Mrs. Sotheby came to see
their daughters who were at the school. Those amiable

people were all kindness and attention, and took me to the hotel where they were staying. They assisted me to look out for some other place of abode, and I was so fortunate as to receive an introduction to an English family of great respectability, who wished for two or three young ladies to board in their house to pursue their studies with the children. This family was that of the Rev. Edward Forster, Chaplain to the British Embassy at the Court of Paris.

Mrs. Forster had four daughters, two grown up and the others eleven and twelve years of age. I liked the appearance of these people, and blessed my good fortune. They were equally prepossessed in my favour, and everything seemed to promise that happiness I so much enjoyed while with them. I found the house always full of the first society. Mr. and Mrs. Forster are both very clever, and every person of celebrity found a welcome reception at their table. There was only one other young lady with me, Miss Dundas, the daughter of Lady Charlotte Dundas, who often used to come to spend the evening with us. The eldest Miss Forster was in England visiting Lord and Lady Nugent, so that Clara, the second daughter, was my companion. They took me to see everything worth notice, and behaved in the kindest manner possible. This was the more welcome to me as neither Mr. nor Mrs. Bray conducted themselves at all well. The former is an ignorant, ill-bred man, and really behaved like a brute when he found I was going to leave his house for one so infinitely more agreeable and respectable.

Fortunately the Forsters lived at the opposite end of the town, therefore I had no intercourse with the Brays.

Mrs. Forster's house was very large, as you will think when I tell you we had six women servants and two men. This is only large in comparison to the Brays'; for I find Newland Hall quite a monster of a dwelling and the men and maids without end. I used to spend the days in seeing sights and the nights either in visiting or receiving company. Everything was mirth and good humour, and I may truly call those my "golden days," for such happiness can surely never be granted to me on earth again.

I must begin now to copy from my journal, for I cannot remember half I have to tell you. One of my first pleasures was a visit to the little town of Vincennes, about three miles out of Paris. There is a fair held in a wood close to this village every year, and we determined to see it for the sake of observing the manners and the customs of the people. We went a large party; took our cold dinner with us and ate it under the shade of some oaks.

The most busy hours for the fair are after it is dark. Numerous coloured lamps were lighted, and all the sports went on with double spirit. There were whirly-go rounds, and shows without end; and among the rest a company of rope-dancers from England. We saw everything and left no place unexplored. Dancing seems indeed the universal delight of the French. Here, as at every other such place, you see large divisions fenced round, and attended by bands of music; for the dances, quadrilles and waltzes are the never-failing sources of pleasure. The country people are dressed in very high caps, ornamented with long flying pieces of muslin and bunches of ribbon streaming from the top; crimson aprons tied with bright green ribbon; very short petticoats. These kind of people dance with great spirit and delight; but the better sort, such as apprentices and milliner's girls, imitate their superiors and scarcely condescend to do more than walk. Some of the young ladies had their fortunes told by a frightful old woman, while the common people flocked round in crowds to laugh at them. I refused, for I thought I had seen enough and felt certain that I could read my fate as well as the old witch before me.

I made a point of paying an early visit to one of the best markets in Paris. This is the market St. Germain; which is held under a very spacious shed, so contrived that the air comes in plentifully from above, and yet the heat is all excluded by an overhanging roof. The confusion of the different materials is very unpleasant to English taste, sight and smell. In one division of the long counters ranged down this place you may see fish; next to it, and quite close, a fine collection of fruit; then comes a row of unfeathered, scranny fowls; and next a huge heap of cabbages, the dying and the dead. Again you see some gay ribbons, gloves, pin cushions, etc., where the purchaser may stand a chance of being regaled by the perfume of a neighbouring assortment of the refuse from every stall in the market.

As I passed down, the people called aloud to each other: "O, look at the great lady; heavens, how tall she is!" You may be sure such observations were not very agreeable, but I was at length accustomed to remarks on my uncommon stature. There are several other places in Paris appropriated for markets, but none are so large as St. Germain.

The public buildings of this far-famed city are certainly very fine. The palaces, churches, and two or three
streets are well worthy a journey from England; but as a
metropolis it should not be compared to our stupendous
London. Paris is only about half the size of our capital,
and its general appearance very far inferior. The streets
are almost all narrow, and universally filthy. This you
will believe when I tell you the channel is in the middle,
and close to the houses is deposited every kind of nui-
sance. Each person forms his own dunghill by the outside of his gate. This is rather coarse language, but it is
literally the case in almost every street. There are no
causeways for foot passengers, who are consequently
splashed with the mud and dirt, and can scarcely
walk three steps in comfort. This in winter is horrible.
But the builders never considered the convenience of the
middle classes, and those who have their carriages at
command care little what becomes of the mobility.

I dare say you have often heard of the boulevards of
Paris. The word signifies bulwarks or outskirts; and
the parts so called consist of very wide streets, paved the
width of eight or ten feet in the middle; and on each side
of this pavement is generally room for two carriages;
then rows of fine large trees, and a very broad walk, with
shops of every possible description on the right and left.
Those places look uncommonly lively at night when all
the shops are lighted, and the splendid coffee-houses
crowded with company. It is the custom to walk on the
boulevards at night in summer. Then the lamps amongst
the trees, the people all in parties, some taking ices,

7

others lounging on chairs, and others walking, form altogether one brilliant scene of enchantment.

This, however, is much more the case in the Palais
Royal; a large building intended originally for a palace
for the royal family; but now used as a number of shops.
It is square and in the middle is a large garden. You
may walk under a continued archway all round, having
the most splendid shops on one hand close to you, and see
the garden through the distances of the pillars which
support the arcade, and enter it whenever you please.
You will easily believe nothing can be more like a fairy
scene, than to see such a place crowded with people in
the midst of the blaze of light from lamps in the shops
and coffee-houses. But I am sorry to add no lady of
modesty can be seen with propriety in this gay scene
after nine o'clock. In the day-time, between two and
five o'clock, it is crowded with genteel society; and when
you have once seen such a place it is sufficient.

The king's palace is situated in the midst of an immense garden open to the public, and which contains
some exquisite statues dispersed among the thick grove
of trees; which pleased me more than anything in the
arrangement of French gardens. For the elegant forms
and pure white marble have such a chaste, quiet beautiful effect; besides, all the classical stories connected with
them make them doubly interesting. The palace is very
spacious and joined to it is the celebrated building called
the Louvre, which contains some of the finest pictures
and statues in the world. When the Emperor Napoleon
conquered any place, his greatest desire was to rob it of
all fine works of art with which he decorated his own

capital, making the galleries of the Louvre the recep-
tacle of everything worth notice; and by that means
he greatly increased the consequence of his metropolis,
for every one who wished to study the fine arts of course
flocked to Paris, to see the master-pieces of ancient artists.
In the Louvre I have spent many, many delightful hours.
I never felt so happy as when wandering among the silent
crowds that decorate this superb place, and only hope I
shall see it again many times before I leave the world.
When Paris was taken by the allied sovereigns, each felt
envious of this exquisite collection, and accordingly every
nation and city was allowed to claim its own. This
might be called strict justice undoubtedly, but in my
opinion it would be of much greater advantage to every
nation if those beautiful specimens of art had been
allowed to remain together; for artists who wish to imitate them now, must go into every kingdom to search for
what before was all to be found in Paris.

The far-famed Church of Notre Dame is not at all
equal to our Minsters. The French look upon it as something almost beyond imagination; but it struck me as
much beneath our buildings of the same description.
There are a number of other fine churches well worthy
notice; but it would be tedious for me to describe them.

Theatres are very numerous, but none equal to our
Drury Lane and Covent Garden. The Opera House is, I
think, larger than ours, but the music much inferior. The
French taste in music does not please me, it is too noisy.
I like the softness of Italian airs a great deal better. I
went to the Italian Opera constantly. I was allowed the
honour of always using the Ambassador's box. At the

French Opera we had Lord Glenlyon's; and when I saw "The Wonderful Lamp," I could scarcely persuade myself but some genii had in reality assisted to arrange the scenery, it was so very beautiful.

One evening I requested Mr. and Mrs. Forster to take me to a masquerade. This was held in the Opera House three nights in the week, the whole of the pit and stage being formed into one large room. You are at liberty to go into any part of the building; and you may be sure such roving about highly pleased me, who have naturally a wish to keep moving into different scenes; and I verily believe if I were not bound by love and Christian duty to stay here I should set off again to-morrow; and then, after all my wanderings were over, I should come home "blind, lame, and comfortless, without a penny in my purse, a poor old maid!!!" But I was talking about the masquerade. Well, I was engaged to two other places of amusement the same evening; so after being at two balls, about two o'clock in the morning, we all slipped on large black silk loose dresses, just like night gowns, over our other clothes; putting black masks and large black hoods on our heads. On entering the theatre you are surrounded with crowds of people dressed like yourself, for it is the fashion to go always in these black dominos; and they chatter to you, and laugh, and make such a buzz it is scarcely possible to imagine where you are come to among so many blackies. I was taken for a gentleman from my height; and consequently several ladies came up to me exclaiming, "Oh! sir, I know who you are," and then told me tales of various fracas they had been in. Music in excellent style is going on all the time, and when you know any party of your friends are to be there it is great amusement to try and find them out.

I early paid a visit to that place so celebrated, called the Louvre. (I find I have already talked of this, so will go to another subject.) There are in Paris a number of delightful public gardens similar to our Vauxhall. To these I went repeatedly. Fireworks form the principal amusement; and then riding in little wooden carriages that go up and down hills with astonishing rapidity. This entertainment is adored by the French, and they flock in crowds to enjoy it. Imagine a circular building round a large space of ground, and one end much lower than the other. Little cars are placed upon it, as on the top of a wide wall, with the wheels sliding in grooves. When seated you are drawn up to the highest part by invisible chains and then come down swift as lightning. Only think how highly honoured I have been by going repeatedly down these wooden mountains with that bewitching poet, Mr. Moore! Do you not feel, yourselves, some degree of pride, that any of your family should have been so gratified? Yes, indeed, I felt prouder than Miss Fanny Fudge when she imagined a count by her side. This dear little man I saw constantly and am half persuaded that my name will be transmitted to posterity along with his; because I had the exquisite pleasure of talking to him; of hearing him talk; of hearing him sing; and of walking many a happy half-hour with him and his sweet children.

Mr. Moore is short, and made compactly like a little doll. He has fine expressive, sparkling grey eyes, a sharp nose, laughing mouth, good teeth, and dimpled chin—

the very essence of good humour; yet occasionally low
spirited. He sings with feeling that would move a heart
of stone; and to hear from his lips his own beautiful song
of "Those Evening Bells," is almost too much to bear.
He is partial to plaintive music, but pleases equally in
gay; for he throws a charm over everything he says or
does. Mrs. Moore is a very beautiful and amiable lady;
and in spite of all the apparent levity of her husband's
mind, perceptible in many of his songs, I think it scarcely
possible for two people to live a life of more perfect
domestic felicity than Mr. and Mrs. Moore. You must
not set me down as "odiously vain," when I tell you this
so celebrated bard used to consider me a great favourite.
This is enough to make me walk two inches taller than
ever. I have a pair of gloves belonging to the dear poet
that are invaluable to me. Fortune favoured me particularly in allowing me to meet with men of celebrity. My
heart has always panted after this kind of society with a
most ardent enthusiasm, and I little thought when seated
in our quiet home at Beverley that I should ever be
gratified as I have been.

It is customary in France for every one to make presents
to their friends on New Year's day; and although I was
alone in the great capital many of my acquaintances
paid me the compliment. Consequently the last day of
the old year is a scene of great bustle. Everybody goes
out to purchase, and all the fashionable places are
crowded. It is supposed that more money is spent in two
or three days, at this season of the year, in sweetmeats
and jewelry than during the whole of the year besides.
The town is like a fair, and every one you meet exclaims,

"What have you bought? oh how beautiful! where did you get it? I must go too," etc., etc. The most favourite shops are those where you can buy a great variety of things for the same price. Some are called shops of five francs; others shops of three francs, where you see all kinds of pretty trifles, and pay the same for each.

About five miles from Paris, on the banks of the Seine, is the village of St. Cloud. Here the king's favourite palace is situated amongst the most beautiful gardens, where I have spent many happy hours rambling from one beauty to another. It was also Napoleon's favourite residence, and from his bed-room window is the most lovely view I have seen.

About twelve miles from Paris is the elegant town of Versailles, containing another large palace and immense gardens. The palace is not occupied, but strangers are allowed to rove over its innumerable apartments, all bare and deserted. The gardens are laid out in beautiful lawns and fine walks, with elegant fountains in every part. These are arranged very fantastically, and when all playing are a beautiful sight. Imagine a number of large basins of water, and in the centre of each groups of figures bearing vases, shells, etc. The water rises from those figures in spouts to an amazing height; and falls in silver showers over them. But I am talking to those who most probably have seen the giant cataract of Niagara, and listened to its mighty moans. Be sure to tell me what you thought on first seeing this exquisite wonder of Nature. We are all *very* anxious to hear from you, indeed. At Versailles I became acquainted with some young ladies who were extremely kind to me, and

with whom I staid many weeks. They are still my correspondents, and one of them my fondly loved friend, whom
I hope to keep as such all my days.

I was on the point of taking a trip into Germany, when
my poor sister requested me to return, that I might take
charge of her little ones. I was disappointed that I
could not effect my purpose, but pleased to show my
affection by giving up my own gratification to her. I
came over last June, and went to see my dear Emily at
Cheltenham, in Gloucestershire. There we staid some
time, and she became evidently worse. We then went
to Malvern in Worcestershire, and afterward to Leamington in Warwickshire; all of these places much recom-
mended for her complaint. We thus passed through a
very beautiful part of England.

While at Leamington I received a letter from my old
school friend, Miss Henniker. Her father had succeeded
to the title and estates of his uncle, and had become the
Rt. Hon. Lord Henniker. She repeated an invitation,
often urged before, that I would go and see her; and
with Emily's permission I accepted. Thus, then, I left
my dear sister at Leamington, and on my way home
made a circuitous route through Norfolk, and staid three
weeks with the Hon. Miss H. and her noble parents. My
lord and lady received me with the kindest attention,
and used every exertion to amuse me. Lord Henniker
used to drive me out in his curricle to see the country,
and Miss H. in her beautiful little gig to see the farmers.
We had fine fun together, and used to set out such a
cavalcade through the park as would have made the
Beverley people actually expire with wonder. Imagine

to yourself a carriage and four, then two or three on single horses, then a chariot, a curricle, a gig and little carriages belonging to the younger branches. All this set off with servants made no little show, and we used to sally forth and visit some distant friends, or gentleman's seat, repeatedly in this way. Lord Henniker has a family of eight children, two of whom are with Miss Sotheby, our former governess. After much brilliant gaiety I returned home to Newland, and found the children much grown.

My poor Emily meanwhile became daily worse and went into Kent, thinking the mild air might restore her. She staid a month with Mrs. Grevis James, and then determined to come home. This was last September, which month she remained with us; and then was so strongly advised to put herself under the celebrated Dr. Bailey, of London, that she endeavoured to summon all her courage and once more part from her dear family. You cannot easily imagine this melancholy scene. We were led to believe it was our last farewell. She was a perfect skeleton, beautiful still, but worn completely away. She shed not a tear, spoke not a word, but sat tranquil as a statue while the poor children kissed her in silent sorrow. I watched her step into the carriage, and thought it was an eternal look I gave her. Thank God, however, good Dr. Bailey has done wonders for her. She was with him six weeks, and then came down to Yorkshire, and is still residing with Dr. Haxby. She promises to come and see her children this spring, and then we must again banish her for the summer. The thought, and constant anxiety for such a family as this, is far too much for her.

In beginning this letter I scarcely knew how or where to begin. In ending it, I scarcely know how or where to end. I often think I would like to get a peep at your home in the wild, wild woods, and see you in your little log cabin, without rooms. How I would enjoy seeing my dear Tom struggling with his dish towels. I would like to hear those wild beasts at their midnight concerts, and I would like to see the mosquitoes and help you fight them.

I think I'll come over and live in your wild country, and milk your cows and be Dolly the maid. Few people would be so happy as I in such a state. Would you take me into your cabin if I wandered across the wide ocean?

God bless you both, my ever beloved brothers, and prosper all your plans. Think of me in your prayers; and believe me fondly your affectionate sister,

MARY SCATCHERD.

CHAPTER VII.

RETURNING to Mr. John Scatcherd and family, it may be again noted that no services of the English Church had been held within or near the township of Nissouri previous to 1824. In the summer of that year the Reverend Mr. McIntosh, a clergyman of the Church of England, held a service on the Proof Line Road of London township, at or near the house of a Mr. Fralick, in the vicinity of what is now known as the village of St. John's. Here Thomas was taken and baptized.

In the summer of 1825, James Newton, the second child, was taken on horseback to Kettle Creek, now St. Thomas, a distance of twenty-six miles, and at the parsonage baptized by the same clergyman. Mr. Scatcherd inquired of the reverend gentleman when he might be expected to hold services at or near Wyton. He replied, "The country is so new, the roads so bad, and my journeys through other parts of the country so long, I could not fix even on a remote day when I could do it." He asked, "Are there not some people near you called Methodists?" "Yes," replied Mr. Scatcherd, "but they go about holding meetings in each others houses, and all seem to be preachers." "Never mind that," said the clergyman; "you had better meet and worship with them, and they will do you good." The advice of the good man was followed, and soon afterwards Mr. Scatcherd and his wife united with the Methodist Church, to which they became ardently attached. In communion with it they lived, governing their religious professions by godly lives, dying in the faith they embraced in early man and womanhood; mourned by a large religious denomination with which they had been identified from its day of small beginnings in the colony, until it has reached an eminence and become a power in the religious world.

In 1824 Mr. Scatcherd brought a span of horses and wagon to the farm; they are said to have been the first used in the western part of the township. He continued clearing and working his land until the year 1830. In December of that year the family removed into, what was then called, The Forks, now the city of London, for the purpose of educating their children. And, further, having brought from the old country what, at that time, was deemed considerable means, and finding no opportunity for investment in a new settlement, Mr. Scatcherd decided to engage in mercantile business. With this object in view, and a stock of goods having been purchased in Hamilton, he opened a dry goods and hardware store on the north side of Dundas street. The banking was then done in Hamilton. Paper having twelve or eighteen months to run was discounted at the rate of six per cent. per annum, and at maturity was, if the maker required, renewed for six or sometimes twelve months.

The penalty for a protested draft in early days, was as severe as the accommodation for discount was liberal. In this connection the following letter will explain itself:

BANK OF UPPER CANADA,
YORK, *29th May, 1823.*

MESSRS. BOULTON & CO.:

Gentlemen: I enclose herewith the draft of John Scatcherd, date 10th December, 1822, on Kay Price and Holman, protested for non-payment, and have accordingly debited your account as follows:

	£	s.	d.
Draft for £100 sterling,	111	2	2
20 per cent. damages,	22	4	5
4 per cent. premium at New York on £120 sterling,	5	6	8
Postage,		5	6
	£138	18	9

I am, gentlemen, your obedient servant,

THOS. G. RIDOUT,
Cashier.

Nearly one-quarter of the protested bill was charged as damages.

In 1830, when Mr. Scatcherd moved to the village plot of London, none of the surveyed township road-lines had been opened. The bush road from Wyton ran through the forest all the distance, except where it passed the clearings of five settlers. Crossing the Wye, it entered the woods on Lot Eleven opposite to where the residence of Mr. William Scatcherd now stands. Continuing through the forest, the traveler forded the Thames river at its intersection with Fourth Concession line of London. Mr. William Guest had a small clearing on the hill. He came into the township in the year 1818. After passing his place, the heavy underbrush of the plains was entered; the track continuing westerly until the river was forded again, sometimes on Lot Eight, sometimes on Lot Nine in Fourth Concession, according to the stage of the water. This was in the vicinity of the Ryan farm, afterwards known as the Killally property. From this point the road returned eastward to Lot Seven, Third Concession.

On Lot Seven, Mr. Robert Webster had settled in 1819. The generous hospitality of this early pioneer was unbounded. Belated travelers, their families and teams were cared for free of charge. The friendly latch-string was always on outside of Robert Webster's door, a standing welcome to all who pulled.

From Lot Seven, the route zigzagged through the woods south, passing Thomas Belton's clearing and crossing the

Governor's road into the Gore near the present toll-gate, between Lots Eight and Nine. Keeping south and westward it passed to the east of where the Great Western Railway workshops, Salter's grove and the cemetery now are, and reached the Governor's road again a few hundred feet east of Adelaide street, opposite the clearing of Noble English; then on to the village still in the forest, until Richmond street was passed. The road ran into the Gore to avoid what was then a large morass, named for many years the Priest's Swamp—a priest having lived on a lot near it on the east. The swamp extended from Salter's grove to the hill at the Asylum grounds. Although now in appearance only a wet piece of land, in those early days cattle entering on it at the east sank out of sight.

The distance from Wyton to London in 1878 is less than nine miles. The bush road was over thirteen miles.

When Mr. Scatcherd settled in Nissouri, July, 1821, the ground where the city of London now stands was an unbroken wilderness, in all its primeval wildness, except in so far as the surveying of London township and Gore gave indication of the approaching civilization. The village plot was surveyed in 1826. Previous to this there was a squatter named Montague on the flats below the forks of the river. His vocation was hunting, trapping, and occasionally ferrying settlers over the

Thames in his canoe. The limits of the first survey were: Wellington street on the east; North street, now Carling, on the north; the river Thames on the south and west. The lots were numbered from Wellington street west.

A few facts, given by one who was an eye-witness when the village consisted of only three structures of any kind, may be of interest to the five-and-twenty thousand people who, at the distance of fifty years, dwell in the beautiful and busy city now covering the meadows and sloping acclivities at the forks of the Thames. Mr. Robert Carfrae claims, and doubtless truly, to have resided longer in London than any now living there. At twenty-three years of age, June, 1827, he came to the surveyed locality, and has resided continuously in village, town and city to the present time, 1878. Mr. Carfrae is a man of intelligence, vigorous in body and mind, and cautious in his statements. The road by which he entered from Westminster crossed the Thames by a bridge at foot of York street. On the hill across the flats, he found Mr. Yerkes and a few men putting up a hewed log-house. This was on northwest corner of Ridout and York streets. In answer to the inquiry: "How far is it to London?" the reply was:, "You are in it." At this time there were only three houses all told, in the village; two of them taverns, the other a court-house and jail.

The first tavern built was on southwest corner of King and Ridout streets. It was a log-house and kept by Peter McGregor. The other tavern was an unfinished frame building, standing on south side of Dundas street, east of Ridout, kept by Abram Carrol. It was burned in the fall of 1827. The well-remembered Mansion House of later days was built on its site.

The court-house and jail was a rough frame structure. It stood between the present court-house and Robinson Hall. In 1828 Peter Vanevery taught school in the upper part. Peter McGregor, the tavern-keeper, was the jailor. During the spring of 1827, a court was held there, said to have been the first which sat in London; and thereafter for some years, a court was held every spring.

The name of the first prisoner confined in the jail was Reed; his offense, stealing an axe, the property of Mr. Dingman, a farmer in Westminster. The criminal was brought into the village and chained to a stump over night, in the tavern yard of the jailor. Next day he was removed to the jail, and chained to a block of wood in one of the unfinished cells. As this was the first known crime committed in the settlement, it created a greater sensation than a murder would now. The heinous enormity of stealing a neighbor's axe, revealed a condition of human depravity in its direst form. None came to The Forks without paying a visit to the jail to see the

8

prisoner. Mr. James Ferguson, present County Registrar, well remembers the prisoner chained to the
block of wood.

Late in December, 1829, this court-house was placed
on runners and drawn by oxen to the southwest corner
of the square, where it still stands and is the only structure of any kind in London now, erected prior to the
summer of 1827. For over half a century it has stood
unharmed by fire, and untouched by the march of
progress, a monument of London in its infancy. Within
the venerable walls of this landmark of early days, the
first court of London was held; the first criminal
sentenced; and the first school taught, which in time
gave way to the Grammar School, the *Alma Mater* of
many boys and girls now in the sere and yellow leaf
of life. And in that house, too, the first divine service
was held. It was used by any denomination wishing
to use it for divine worship.

The first burying-ground was situate on the west
side of Ridout, between Dundas and North, now Carling
street. It belonged to the Church of England. In that
ground all were buried, including the cholera cases of
1832. On this burial lot, opposite the present court-
house, a frame was put up in 1828, intended as a place
of worship by the Church of England. This was the
first effort at church building. The frame was taken
down, put up again, finished and used as a place of

worship, known as St. Paul's Church. On Ash Wednesday, 1844, it was burned. The Cathedral, built on the same ground, was dedicated Ash Wednesday, 1846.

The Methodists put up, finished, and possessed the first place of worship in the village, a frame building plastered on the outside. It stood on the northwest corner of North (now Carling) and Ridout streets.

In 1827 Mr. Goodhue, afterwards the Honorable G. J. Goodhue, kept a store in Westminster, on the First Concession, two miles from London. There the villagers did their purchasing. No goods were sold in London at that time, excepting the sales made by Dennis O'Brien, a peddler, from his wagon on the Court-house Square. During the year 1828 Mr. O'Brien took possession of a vacant blacksmith's shop, placed some rough boards on barrels for a counter, and there opened and kept the first store in London. He had also a store house. It was without chinking. Through wide spaces between the logs, inquisitive eyes outside could observe the kinds and quantities of goods within. They were principally long-handled frying-pans, baking-kettles, griddles and spiders—the latter a cross between a frying-pan and baking-kettle. This incipient store was on south side of Dundas street, Lot 18, and was occupied for trade until a store and dwelling-house were built on the same lot; to which the goods were transferred before any other place of merchandise was opened. One or two small places for sale of goods followed, but did not last long.

In 1830 Mr. Goodhue moved his store from Westminster to the northeast corner of Ridout and Dundas streets; and in October of the same year Mr. John Jennings opened a store on Ridout near King street. Early in the winter of 1831 Mr. John Scatcherd opened a store on lot 18, north side of Dundas street. This was the fourth place of trade deserving the name of store. At that time the population did not exceed two hundred. The village was active and grew fast. Lots were taken up and cleared; houses, frame and log, were built, though many of them were not finished for years.

The post-office, in 1827, was kept in Westminster, on the First Concession, not far from Mr. Goodhue's store, at a tavern where the stage running between Toronto and Detroit changed horses. In the latter part of 1828 it was moved to Ira Schofield's house, on his farm, a few hundred feet east of the convent on Dundas street. Mr. Schofield was postmaster. Later Mr. Goodhue was appointed, and kept it on the east side of Ridout street, near Dundas. Mr. John Harris succeeded Mr. Goodhue, and kept the office at his house on Ridout street for some time. Mr. Goodhue, being reappointed, transferred the office to the store of Goodhue & Lawrason, on northwest corner of Dundas and Ridout streets. In 1842 Mr. Good-

hue removed it to the east end of old Robinson Hall.
He then built a one-story brick post-office north of and
close to the residence of Dr. Anderson, west side of Ridout street. This building was destroyed by fire, and the
post-office kept a short time in the lower part of the
American Hotel property, east side of Ridout street, opposite Court-house Square. It was removed from there
to the Royal Exchange, near the northwest corner of
Dundas and Ridout streets. From there the post-office
business was removed in 1860 to the present commodious
building on Richmond street, Mr. Lawrence Lawless suc-
ceeding Mr. Goodhue as postmaster.

The rate of postage between Canada and Great Britain
was, in 1822, the following: The inland rate was sixpence
sterling for the first hundred miles, with twopence added
for every additional hundred miles, plus the packet rate
of one shilling sterling. A single letter from London
therefore cost: London to Quebec, one shilling and twopence; Quebec to Halifax, one and sixpence; Halifax to
Britain, one shilling; total, three shillings and eight pence
sterling, equal to ninety-two cents.

A single letter consisted of one piece of paper; double
letter, two pieces, and so on.

The first bank established in London was the Bank of
Upper Canada, on Ridout near King street, in 1832 or
1833. The first magistrate was Ira Schofield and Mr.
John Scatcherd was the second. The first lawyer was

Mr. Timbrook, who came to the village in 1833. The London *Sun* was first newspaper, beginning in 1832, edited by Mr. Edward Allen Talbot. The *Gazette* was second newspaper, edited by Mr. Hodgkinson

Mr. Carfrae came from Toronto to assist in building the present court-house. He found the square cleared, and men engaged grubbing out stumps, preparing for the foundation. William Hale came from Toronto to burn the bricks. Part of them were burned near Court-house Square; the remainder on Walter Nixon's farm, now part of Petersville. The structure was built fronting west. After the foundation was laid Mr. Heward, the contractor, remonstrated with the commissioners against putting up the building with its rear towards the village, and offered to stand the expense of making the changes if the commissioners would consent. One of them obstinately refused, and insisted on no change being made. He carried his point, and the court-house was built with its back upon London. It was finished in 1830. An interest in lands down the river was said to have been the cause of this obstinacy.

The first execution in the village was that of C. A. Burley, in 1830, for shooting a constable.

In 1830 Dundas street was cut out to Wellington. East of Richmond street, there was a swamp making Dundas street impassable, except in winter when frozen. Travelers coming into the village from the east kept on the high land north of Dundas street around the swamp. An excavation made on Dundas street near Ridout, in 1876, uncovered an oak stump, the top of it four feet six inches below the grade of the street. At this point there was seven feet of filling over the original surface of the ground. A portion of this oak stump is now in posses- sion of the County Registrar, a memento of primitive London.

At London the first opportunity of sending the chil- dren to school being found, Thomas and James became pupils at the school of Miss Stimson.

In the summer of 1831, Mr. Scatcherd went to Eng- land on business connected with his father's estate. His route was by Erie Canal on a packet boat to Schenec- tady, and from there to Albany on the first east-bound passenger train over the first railroad built in New York State.

The business in London was successfully carried on during five years. But Mr. Scatcherd finding that the life of a storekeeper in a village did not suit his taste, returned to the farm.

Before those events took place Mr. Thomas Scatcherd had purchased lands adjoining his brother, and had cleared a large portion of his farm. Their houses were separated only by the Wye, and as the brothers had married sisters the family relations were doubly intimate. They united their means and built a grist-mill, saw-mill, woolen factory and tannery; all very desirable in a new

country. While Mr. Scatcherd was in London the first
log school-house had been built. It was situate on the
Side Road, eastern portion of the West Half of Lot VI,
First Concession of Nissouri, two and a half miles distant from Wyton. To that school such of the children
as were old enough to walk so far were sent, except
Thomas.

Referring to the early settlement of Nissouri, Rev. Dr.
Webster writes:

"When Mr. Scatcherd came into the township it was
almost an unbroken wilderness. His brother Thomas
joined him in the following year, 1822, and found fields
of wheat, oats, and corn, well advanced. The Messrs.
Scatcherd soon adapted themselves to bush life. They
hired men to assist in chopping and clearing and quickly
had cultivated farms. In this way they helped the other
settlers very much; not only by circulating money, but
by furnishing that which was better than money, wheat
and corn. The Scatcherds, like all pioneers, had their
privations and struggles; but having means at command
did not suffer for necessaries when these could be purchased, which, however, could not always be done."

Rev. Thomas Brown, Nissouri, an early settler, says:
"The Scatcherds came into Nissouri in 1821 and
1822. They were a wonder and astonishment to the
more hardy and robust settlers.

"The idea of young gentlemen like them who had learned to farm by rule, undertaking to contend with the difficulties and hardships of backwoods life and make farms out of the wilderness, seemed preposterous in the extreme. All predicted that after a short time the young Englishmen would give up and return to England, minus their money and disgusted with the country. We were greatly mistaken in such predictions, and surprised to see how quickly they adapted themselves to their surroundings. By an untiring energy, and judicious use of their money, they took the lead in the settlement and had the first grain and provisions for sale. By the year 1830 they had their lands well cleared and fenced; the stumps out of some of the fields, and frame barns erected.

"The training and experience the young men received during their apprenticeship inured greatly to their advantage, and was turned to practical account. Straight fences and straight furrows seemed the rule; none of us could equal their ploughing. They stocked their farms with improved breeds of horses, cows and sheep. In this way they conferred lasting benefits on the neighbourhood. Ever ready and willing to extend a helping hand; ever kind and obliging, they were considered an acquisition to the neighbourhood and country, and were accorded the first place in the hearts of all who knew them."

As the population in the township increased, Mr. Scatcherd was early appointed a magistrate; and when the benefits of municipal institutions were granted, he was among the first elected. He served his township and county as Councillor, Reeve, Warden, and Superintendent of Education. He held those positions for many years, when Nissouri township formed part of the county of Oxford; and afterwards when it was set off to Middlesex.

During the construction of the Great Western Railway, Mr. Scatcherd represented his county as one of the Board of Directors for that road.

In loyalty to his sovereign and country he stood second to no man. During the misgovernment of the province which culminated in the rebellion, he was firm and un-flinching in favor of constitutional government. In every constitutional way within his power he opposed and vig-orously denounced all those in office who, under the guise of loyalty, oppressed the people. His name ap-pearing on a petition calling attention to existing griev-ances and asking relief, was a pretext for omitting him from the list of magistrates contained in a new commis-sion at that time issued. But that was not the real cause of offense. Mr. Scatcherd's independence and uncompro-mising opposition to wrongs daily increasing, and for which no redress could be had, made him distasteful to those who were misgoverning the country. He was not dismissed, there being no offense alleged; the omission of his name in the new commission was the farthest they could go, and exhibited the high-handed partizan spirit of the time.

Before that occurred Mr. Scatcherd had received the nomination, and was the Reform candidate for London. This, according to a leading journal, was the cause of dropping his name from the Commission of the Peace and Court of Requests.

Electoral Address.

To the Electors of the Town of London :

Gentlemen : From a deep sense of duty to my country, and at your kind and frequent solicitations, I offer myself a candidate for your suffrages at the ensuing election.

In thus coming forward I would say, that should you elect me as your Representative, I shall endeavour, as far as I am able, to support every measure that may tend to the good of your town, and zealously advocate every principle of Reform on which I consider the happiness and prosperity of our country depends.

I am, gentlemen,

Your obed't serv't,

John Scatcherd.

London, *June 10th, 1836.*

At close of the polls Colonel Burwell, the opposing candidate, was successful. The omission of Mr. Scatcherd's name from the magistracy led to newspaper commentaries, both in Canada and in the States. An act of injustice by Sir Francis Bond Head, representing England, was magnified in republican America, and used in distempered party controversy to alarm the United States about an impending Van Buren monarchy.

Extract from the Cincinnati Whig and Commercial Intelligencer.

In some parts of this country it is evident that there is a strong disposition, on the part of a portion of our fellow-citizens, the Van Burenites, for the establishment of a monarchical goverment under a Kinderhook dynasty. As it is desirable that the advocates of such a system should occasionally obtain a little knowledge of the measures pursued under monarchical and arbitrary governments, we have annexed an extract from a recent Canadian journal for their guidance; so they may have some idea how matters proceed where the people have no voice, and where their wishes are as little regarded as if they were the most abject slaves; where an upright, honest, public officer is sure to be objectionable to the minions who pander to the powers that be, so long as they are fed and pampered for their pliant but contemptible subserviency.

[The following was copied from the *Journal*, then a leading paper in Western Canada.]

By the arrival of last Thursday's mail from Toronto the good people of this town received the important information that his honour Judge Young, has been elevated to the situation of Commissioner of the Court of Requests, *vice* John Scatcherd, Esq., dismissed for having had the temerity to allow himself to be put in nomination for the representation of the town of London, at the last election. This information has been quite unexpected, and has created a degree of excitement which will not soon be allayed.

Mr. Scatcherd is an old and respected magistrate, esteemed by all who know him as a man of unbending integrity and sound judgment; and we believe it may be safely said that there exists not in the Province a man who has fewer enemies or more friends. Retired in his habits, unassuming in his manners, he may not have attracted much the smiles, or the adulation of upstart snobs, but in the estimation of thinking men who look beneath the surface of human life, he stands deservedly high, and by such men is regarded as a most valuable member of society. Whigs and Tories, Radicals and Republicans, all unite in declaring that a more conscientious, more upright, a more independent, or more mild and impartial magistrate never sat upon the Bench of the London District.

Mr. Scatcherd came to this country about seventeen years ago, with what in those days was esteemed a princely fortune. He has since, almost annually, received remittances from England, his native country, and has expended every shilling which he has obtained in the improvement of the country, and in alleviating the sorrows of many a broken heart. And he is now, no doubt by the request or by the influence of some upstart official, dismissed from an office, in discharging the duties of which he gave to all parties the utmost possible satisfaction.

As far as regards Mr. Scatcherd himself His Excellency has doubtless conferred a favor of no inconsiderable magnitude; but the country feels—deeply feels—the loss of his valuable services; and the people with one accord regard his dismissal as an act of petty tyranny which plainly conveys to them that from henceforth no independent man can hold office of any kind without risk of arbitrary dismissal. Cardinal Wolsey is represented as saying: "Had I served God as faithfully as I have my King, He would not have deserted me in my old age." And Mr. Scatcherd may say in a more noble and infinitely less repentant spirit: "Had I served Sir Francis Bond Head half as zealously as I have my adopted country, he would not have cast me off as one of the lost sheep of the House of Kent."

Sir Francis has displayed more political acumen than he got credit for. However much the death of William the Fourth, our illustrious sovereign, may be deplored, it is an event which from His Majesty's advanced age and impaired constitution may ere long occur, then another election takes place. His Excellency and the offical gang are now engaged trying what effects intimidation may produce on the minds of the people. The weak and the timid, the vascillating and the ignorant will doubtless be more or less affected by such a system.

The people in this part of the country intend to address ·Mr. Scatcherd, congratulating him on dismissal from an office which in some degree identified him with a base, corrupt and vindictive administration.

Although party feeling ran high in those days and was very bitter, yet, as already stated, no word nor act of Mr. Scatcherd was adduced, nor alleged, capable of being construed into disloyalty. In the year 1840, a new Commission of the Peace was issued, and his name gazetted. The following letter came officially:

CLERK OF THE PEACE OFFICE,

WOODSTOCK, *10th March, 1840.*

Sir: I have this day received the Commission of the Peace for the District of Brock, and have the honour to inform you that your name appears there as a Magistrate for the said District. I have the honour to be, sir,

Your obedient servant,

W. LAPENETIERE.

JOHN SCATCHERD, Esq., Nissouri, London.

During the spring of the year 1849, Squire Scatcherd,
with some members of his family, went on a visit to Mr.
Wesley Freeman's near Simcoe, where his daughter Jane
was then spending a few weeks. Stopping at Dorman's
tavern on the Burford road for dinner, he noticed a saw-
mill not far distant, stocked with large, fine-looking pine
logs. An examination of the mill led to inquiry respecting the property connected with it. Four hundred acres
of well-timbered pine land; and fifty acres on which the
mill, a fine dwelling, store, and several other houses were
built, all made a desirable-looking investment, provided it
were for sale and the price suited. It was found the
mill and lands belonged to the Crapo estate, and were
in the market. A short correspondence led to a purchase
of the property.

Soon after, Mr. Scatcherd took up his residence on this
newly-acquired possession. A few weeks were spent in
repairing and putting the saw-mill in order. The day
fixed for starting arrived. For the first cut two logs were
selected as an average of the whole, because on the quality of the logs depended the value of the purchase. The
two logs were placed in position on the carriages and
securely fastened. The steam valve was opened, and off
went the machinery, the wheels spinning like tops and
the belts running swiftly. The mill was of excellent construction, and in the best of order. The saws seemed to
dance with delight, as they tossed the rich yellow saw-

dust in the air.   On removing the slabs one or two dark-colored knots were visible; and as each board thereafter came off the knots increased in number and blackness. Mr. Scatcherd watched the cutting of these logs with much anxiety, until they were finished.   Finding the knots increased in number and blackness, he became disgusted; turned around to his son James and said: " Here, my lad, take the mill and do what you like with it; I have had enough."

After which he left the mill and logs, and returned to his farm.   The fact was, the logs were not as good as they appeared to be; they turned out too much poor common lumber, and too little clear stuff to make saw-milling profitable.   The mill was run for one year, stocked with a new lot of logs, and then sold to Messrs. De Blaquiere & Elwes, of Woodstock, at an advance over the first cost.   There was also a small profit on the lumber cut.

Dismissing Burford and the saw-mill from his mind, Mr. Scatcherd took delight in the cultivation of his farm. Country life had many fascinations for him.   He was restless and impatient for frost and snow to disappear.   In early spring he offered rewards to whoever would show him the first robin, or bluebird.   To him the coming spring was a source of inspiration.   The first notes of early songsters, the first peeping blade of grass and budding flower, gave him intense pleasure.   At that season he arose with the dawn and walked about his fields. The forest enrobing itself in its summer dress; the blossoming flowers and shrubs; the growing crops and waving grain, were year by year a recurring exhilaration and delight to him. "Give me," he used to say, "the bud, the blossom, and the full-grown leaf."

For him, the maturing harvest-field had a charm and a prophecy above and beyond the yield of grain.

From beginning of spring to autumn, his spirits were joyously exuberant. But the fading and falling leaves gave his mind a tinge of sadness, and winter was a dreary and dismal prison.

There are few events in the routine of a farmer's occupation worthy of noting. Planting and harvesting followed by winter, season after season, leaves but little of interest to record.

Mr. Scatcherd's time was fully taken up with his official duties of township and county, managing his mills, cultivating his farm and beautifying it with ornamental trees. The evergreen grove in front of his dwelling bears witness to his taste and success in tree-planting. When through the tops of those waving pines the soft winds murmur, it seems as if John Scatcherd was walking beneath them once more.

The Squire's services as magistrate were frequently called for, and always reluctantly performed. He exceedingly disliked hearing and determining cases between

9

neighbors, and would not do so until all efforts at per-
suading them to settle their differences were exhausted.

In the year 1854 Mr. Scatcherd was prevailed upon to
accept the nomination as Reform Candidate for the West
Riding of Middlesex. At close of the polls, having
received a majority of the votes, he was declared duly
elected.

Mr. Scatcherd represented the West Riding of Middlesex in Parliament to the close of his life, enjoying the fullest confidence of his constituents. He took an active
part in the debates of the day with a hearty earnestness.
On all measures coming up before the House he followed
his own convictions, whether agreeing with the party or
otherwise. Always in his seat, he never avoided the
responsibility of having his vote recorded. Squire
Scatcherd was a man of the people, from the people, and
legislated for the people.

In politics he was an Independent Reformer, and while
true to the principles of the body with whom he was associated, would never acknowledge the party whip. He
entered into his electioneering campaigns with energy
and earnestness. As a public speaker he had not the
practice of eloquent or florid oratory; but in dealing with
his subjects evinced a warm, manly, honest frankness, that
carried conviction. This made him a welcome speaker;
always insuring a respectful and attentive audience.

During the years he served as Member of Parliament, Mr. Scatcherd formed an acquaintance with Dr. R. Basil Church, who represented the county of Grenville. Their mutual appreciation ripened to an intimacy exceeding what is usually termed friendship. They lived in the same hotel, had their rooms near together, waited for each other at meals, went in company to the Parliament house, sat up for each other when either returned late, parted reluctantly when they retired for the night, and greeted each other in the morning as if they had been separated for months. Each wrote constantly to his own family concerning the other in terms of praise and tenderness. Yet, notwithstanding all this affection, they were as far apart in politics as an ultra-Conservative and unchanging Reformer could be. They were as far opposed to each other in religious views as thorough Methodist and zealous Universalist ever were. In person also, their dissimilarity was striking. While 'absolutely the opposite of each other in some seemingly essential characteristics, they were one and inseparable in all else.

In the last session of the Canadian Parliament at Toronto, winter of 1857–'58, the first indications of failing health appeared in Mr. Scatcherd. His previous electioneering campaign occurred in December, 1857. The contest was close and spirited; party feeling ran high; his exposure to inclement weather; long weary journeys undertaken over roads in their worst condition; addressing meetings frequently twice a day, with the attendant excitement, causing him loss of sleep—these toils were too much for his physical strength.

Parliament assembled soon after the election. He took his seat in the House, and although with health somewhat impaired, attended to the duties as usual. In the latter part of the session he received a shock which affected him very injuriously.

One bright and unusually genial afternoon in March, 1858, as he and Dr. Church were conversing together, the latter said: "Well, Scatcherd, I will go upstairs and write a letter to my wife," and immediately left for that purpose. A few minutes later Col. Playfair, a brother member, came into the room and inquired for Dr. Church. "He has just gone upstairs to write a letter," replied Mr. Scatcherd. The Colonel went directly upstairs and saw Dr. Church resting his head upon his arms on the table, apparently asleep. After pausing a moment, he said: "Church, are you asleep?" Receiving no reply, the question was repeated. No response being given, Playfair advanced to Dr. Church, and was shocked to find him dead. The Doctor had only written half a dozen lines, the last words being: "I fear that poor Scatcherd will not last out another yea——." The word "year" was not completed. Life had fled! Thus, peacefully and instantly, and no doubt painlessly, the strong and vigorous man, the dearly beloved and constant associate, entered upon the sleep that knows no earthly waking, his last thoughts (perhaps the cause of the crisis) being full of tenderness and solicitude for his ailing friend.

As might be expected, the shock touched every fiber and nerve of Mr. Scatcherd's being. He rallied from it, but never recovered.

His family being informed of the sad incident and of his condition, took him home, where the pure air, familiar scenery and association with his affectionate kindred and numerous friends seemed, for a short time, to revive him. But his strength gradually failed. Although his nervous prostration increased, and culminated in paralysis, he lingered until June; when in his fifty-ninth year he breathed his last, with a sure and steadfast hope of a glorious immortality.

The public announcement of Mr. Scatcherd's death was received with expressions of deepest sorrow wherever the widely-esteemed name was known. The United Legislature of Canada East and Canada West, then in session at Toronto, adjourned in testimony of respect for the deceased member; the Conservative French Canadian leader of the East, Hon. G. Etienne Cartier, sustaining the motion for adjournment made by the Reform leader of the West, Hon. George Brown.

From the Toronto Globe.

ANNOUNCEMENT OF MR. SCATCHERD'S DEATH TO PARLIA-
MENT—THE HOUSE ADJOURNS.—On Wednesday, the 15th inst.,
the melancholy intelligence of Mr. Scatcherd's demise was
announced to the House of Assembly, of which he was a
worthy member, as follows:

The Speaker stated that he had received a letter from the
son of the deceased, intimating that John Scatcherd, Esq.,
Member for the West Riding of Middlesex, had died:

LONDON, *June 15, 1858.*

The Hon. the Speaker of the Legislative Assembly:

SIR: I regret to inform you that my father, John Scatcherd, Member for
the West Riding of Middlesex, died this day at twelve o'clock.

Your obedient servant,

THOMAS SCATCHERD.

Mr. Brown then rose and said: I am sure, Sir, that the
announcement you have just made must have caused deep
pain to many of the members of this House. Mr. Scatcherd's
illness may have prevented his being personally known to
gentlemen who this session for the first time have taken their
seats in this House—but by no member who sat with him in
last Parliment, by no one who learned to know him as I did,
and to appreciate the sterling character and kind heart of my
deceased friend, can the announcement of his death have
been received without deep emotion. Mr. Scatcherd was one
of the oldest and most respected settlers of the Western section
of Upper Canada.

A native of England, he came to Canada very many years
ago, and after encountering and overcoming the usual trials
of the early pioneers of the forest, he gradually rose by the
uprightness and manly force of his character to a position
of great influence in his locality, and finally to be known and
esteemed throughout the Province. For many years he took
a leading part in the municipal affairs of the county of Oxford,

occupying with credit to himself and advantage to his constituents the office of Warden of the county; and when, by a new arrangement. of the electoral divisions, his section of the county was thrown into Middlesex, Mr. Scatcherd became Warden of that county, and finally Representative in Parliament of the West Riding. In all these capacities my deceased friend won the esteem and respect of all who came in contact with him.

As a member of this House, Mr. Scatcherd pursued the same straightforward course that distinguished him through life. Punctual in the discharge of every duty, and thoroughly conversant with the business before the House, he was ever ready to give a firm and intelligent verdict on the side he, in his conscience, conceived to be right. I doubt, Sir, if there is any public man who has earned for himself a higher character for uprightness and fidelity as a representative than has John Scatcherd. He was truly an honest man. I move, Mr. Speaker, "That out of respect to the memory of the late John Scatcherd, Esq., a member of this House, the House do now adjourn."

Hon. Attorney-General Cartier seconded the motion.

The House then adjourned.

From the London Free Press, Friday Morning, June 18, 1858.

THE LATE JOHN SCATCHERD, ESQ., M. P. P.—The decease of Mr. John Scatcherd, the member for the Riding of West Middlesex, though expected for some time past, has excited the regrets of all who knew him personally, or were acquainted with his course as a public man. His health had been somewhat feeble during the winter, and the excitement and fatigue consequent upon the parliamentry election in December last tended greatly to impair it still further. Staunch to the performance of the trust reposed in him by the noble constituency whose political sentiments he represented, he did not fail to present himself in his seat in the House at the commencement of the present session, when prudence would, perhaps, have counseled less active pursuits, at least till his health had become firmer. But while attending to his parliamentary duties, a circumstance occurred which greatly shook his nervous system, and from the effects of which he never recovered—we refer to the sudden death of Dr. Church.

Mr. Scatcherd was an Englishman, and emigrated from his native county of York nearly thirty years ago. At that time this portion of the Province was a dense forest, and the pioneers of civilization had to go through many a trial and hardship, of which few can now have an adequate idea. But the indomitable will and unremitting industry of men like the subject of our sketch have blessed it with fertility. The sterling qualities of Mr. Scatcherd soon won for him the regard of his fellows, and we find him rising from a township councilor and reeve to be warden of the county of Oxford, which honorable position he occupied with great credit for some time.

Subsequently, the territorial boundaries of the counties of Oxford and Middlesex were altered, and Nissouri West, in which Mr. Scatcherd lived, was thrown into the county of Middlesex. Here, again, Mr. Scatcherd's well-known character soon enabled him to take his seat as warden of this county, and when the parliamentary election of 1854 came on, he was selected by a convention, held at Strathroy, as the candidate in the Reform interest, and was triumphantly placed at the head of the poll by his numerous and enthusiastic friends. The performance of his political duties was one unswerving path of rectitude, and he earned for himself a place in the hearts of the people which was recently illustrated by his second return to Parliament by an increased majority, and in the face of an opposition that was sustained by government influences.

In his private capacity, Mr. Scatcherd may be said to have been a model man. His honor was unsullied; his industry constant; his fidelity to his friend unshaken.   As a neighbor, he was kind, obliging and considerate, and many have cause to remember, with gratitude, kindnesses received at his hands. Such a man cannot pass away, without exciting much deep-felt regret, and, even those who have only known him by name, cannot remain unmoved when they know that an early and industrious settler, a kind neighbor, a beloved father, a faithful public servant, and a staunch representative of public opinion, has been taken from among us.   May his example stimulate the young to fitting exertions, while his success, in private as well as public life, serves to illustrate the rewards which, in a free and fruitful country like Canada, so frequently await those who tread an honorable path, such as was pressed by the feet of John Scatcherd.

After this editorial, the *Free Press* concluded the obituary as follows:

THE FUNERAL.—At one o'clock yesterday afternoon, a very large number of the relatives and friends assembled at the beautiful residence of the late Mr. Scatcherd, on the Second Concession of Nissouri West.

The house was soon filled, and a vast number could not gain admittance.   The Reverend Mr. Foreman, Wesleyan Minister, commenced the religious services by singing and prayer; after which he preached a most impressive sermon from the 24th chapter of Matthew and 44th verse: "Therefore be ye also ready; for in such an hour as ye think not, the Son of Man cometh."

About two o'clock the coffin was removed from the house to the hearse by the pall-bearers amidst the tears of the family, and the cortege moved slowly down the beautiful walk leading from the house to the road.   We could form no conception of the number of carriages, teams, etc., which were there until the procession had all got into line on the road.   Then it might be seen what a rare number of people had come from every part of the country to pay the last tribute of respect to all that was mortal of John Scatcherd. There were upwards of one hundred carriages, etc., besides a large number of horsemen.

A pleasing feature of the funeral was, that men of all political proclivities, and religious creeds, met on common ground and testified by their presence to the worth of the deceased.

The place of interment is situated about two miles from Wyton on a beautiful eminence. And on the summit of that eminence were interred the remains of the deceased, in sure and certain hope of a glorious resurrection.

To this may be added that : In the mournful procession a great number of warm friends and former supporters from the West Riding took part.

Seven years later, all but a month, the family mourned the death of their dearly beloved mother. She died on seventeenth of May, 1865 — called hence to meet her husband in that land where parting never comes. If a pure Christian life, consistent kindness and benevolence, accompanied by a faith that never faltered and a hope that never dimned, could render their possessor immortal, then surely immortality is hers. Her biography, her Christian life, and her many virtues, are written in the hearts of her children and of those who knew her best. Her remains repose alongside those of her husband ; a granite monument marking the last earthly resting-place of John and Anne Scatcherd, on Robins' Hill, West Nissouri.

John and Anne Scatcherd reared a family of twelve children, who all received a liberal education, two of them being fitted for such professional life as was most congenial to their taste.

The names of the children were: Thomas, James Newton, Emily, John, Jane, Robert Colin, George, William, Lavinia, Anne, Mary Eleanor and Harry.

Eight lived to mourn the loss of the kind-hearted and dearly beloved father in 1858; the dearly beloved and kind-hearted mother in 1865; both of whom when they died left to their offspring an ever-enduring legacy—their upright and unspotted moral and Christian character.

As a man of business Mr. Scatcherd did not enter into doubtful speculations; nor did he hoard money. But having brought with him from England an amount of funds which he invested in land, and in improvements, the estate was from time to time enlarged by new purchases, and additional value given to every acre through judicious culture and general good management. And Wyton, his home in the deep forest wilderness, was transformed to be the beautiful center of fruitful orchard gardens, and bountiful farm fields.

In him the poor always had a friend; and while never intrusive, the benefit of his best judgment and advice was readily given to those who sought it; and it was often sought.

Mr. Scatcherd's personal appearance was pleasingly striking. He was five feet eleven inches high, well made. Had a light step and graceful movement. Hair jet black, high massive forehead, eyes gray. Complexion dark rather than fair. Prominent features, indicating strength and decision of character. A hearty infectious laugh, that warmed and spread like sunshine. His voice was full, and in tone pleasing. In conversation he was exceedingly agreeable. When in society with him, a magnetism irresistible was felt. The pleasure young or old enjoyed in his company during an afternoon's drive was not soon forgotten. Formal visits, or parties, he disliked; his greatest social enjoyment being around his own fireside with old friends. At such times the hours would pass often unnoticed until after midnight. Extremely fond of singing, he engaged in it himself, and encouraged his children to join him.

When Squire Scatcherd returned home from a trip of pleasure or business, he always brought a budget of news for the instruction or amusement of the family, which he would relate in a peculiarly fascinating manner. Beginning with everything in the order of its occurrence, and continuing to the end, he gave what was seen and heard during his absence. Hour after hour would be spent in relating these gleanings of every-day occurrences; he never seeming to get weary, and the family never tired of hearing. It appeared impossible for him to go anywhere, or be in any place, without picking up something worthy of notice. Connected with all he told were running comments, inciting his hearers to emulate that which was deemed worthy, or to detest and despise all that was deserving of censure. The impressions thus made on the children for good could not be over-estimated. It was certainly an excellent mode of teaching. It stimulated observation, instructed the mind, strengthened the memory, and led to order in arranging, digesting and narrating.

In the government of his family he was firm, and might be termed a strict disciplinarian. Among his children a word was law; but no sense of fear accompanied the father's presence. There was nothing stern, but much earnestness in his manner. He fully appreciated the desire and necessity for recreation and amusement, and entered into the various sports and pastimes of his children with almost boyish avidity. He seemed to take it for granted that delinquencies and shortcomings might be expected; and when coming fully and squarely under his notice, were dealt with promptly and effectively; but he never put himself on a committee of discovery to pry into or find out the faults and mistakes of his children. A tale-bearer he despised. Any one bringing complaints was soon given to understand, and were made to feel, they had undertaken a thankless mission.

A home thus ruled and governed could not be, and was not, other than one of domestic happiness. The influence of it is still felt in annually drawing the children and grandchildren to the old homestead; where each recurring Christmas finds them assembled around a happy fireside, perpetuating and keeping green the memory of those parents whose highest gratification on earth was the happiness of their children.

In his public career Mr. Scatcherd emulated the example of his honored father. His course was one of plain, unswerving rectitude. His principles were not founded on the shifting sands of party politics; nor did they vary with the hope of profit or prospect of preferment. He did not set his sentiments by the weathercock. The idea of fair-play and honesty was paramount in all his thoughts; and characterized every act in all relations of life.

CHAPTER VIII.

MR. THOMAS SCATCHERD OF LONDON, BARRISTER-AT-LAW, QUEEN'S COUNSEL, AND MEMBER OF PARLIAMENT FOR THE NORTH RIDING OF THE COUNTY OF MIDDLESEX.

ON a preceding page it is seen that Thomas Scatcherd was born on the tenth of November, 1823; and that in his eighth year the family removed into London, which circumstance furnished the first opportunity for the boy to attend school. He had been accustomed to attend a Sunday class which assembled in his own home at Wyton, his mother superintendent and teacher. In that class were four besides himself, brother and sister. One came a mile; one, two miles, and two others, five miles. Two of these scholars are now business men in London. Soon after arriving in the then village of The Forks, otherwise London, Thomas Scatcherd became a pupil at the school taught by Miss Stimson. One who was then a scholar there has described the place and incident. He says:

"On the morning of the day Thomas made his first appearance at a public school, he was the last pupil to enter the room. A wide fire-place occupied a space in the wall opposite the door. There were no jambs on either side;

but midway between hearth and ceiling the branch of a
tree sprang from the wall. By accident it had grown in a
curve, and been hewn down and shaped to symmetrical
form. The interior of the curve was filled with clay, the
same material occupying spaces between the logs of
which the humble edifice was constructed. On one side
of the room a long desk extended, which the pupils occupied in turn for writing. Besides this, small forms were
arranged near the fire-place for the scholars; while a chair,
conveniently placed for the matron of this incipient educational establishment, completed its furniture. The nar-
rator of the scene occupied the second form from the
front; and more for the pleasure of enjoying his new slate
and pencil than for improvement, was experimenting over
pot-hooks, straight lines and curves. The fire was all
aglow, and imparted an air of comfort to the quietude
just beginning to settle over the twenty-five or thirty children in the room, when the door opened, and the youth,
who was subsequently Member for Middlesex, entered.
Comfortably clothed in well-shaped garments, his figure
impressed the memory where it still survives. The legs
were short, the body compact, and the head large, having
on it short-cut hair. His face was grave and demeanour
suggestive of thought and care. He walked sedately forward, and, under the influence of daily instruction at
home and the lessons taught in the Wyton Sunday-
school, knelt down and prayed. It was not as other chil-

dren did, then or since. The lessons of his mother blossomed in the boy and ripened in the future public citizen. Thomas took his seat directly in front of the writer. After the period of early pupilage our pursuits were cast in different lines. We met occasionally in advanced boyhood only to compare notes in accessions of elementary knowledge. Subsequently to this, when on his way to Parliament, we sometimes had opportunities to meet and talk of past and present."

Miss Stimson had the honor of founding the first lady's school taught in London. She was a kind-hearted teacher, forbearing with the wayward, and patient with the dull. Yet, notwithstanding her gentleness and kindness of heart, discipline was often necessary. Her severest and most dreaded punishment was pinning the boys to her dress! This was considered worse than ferule or birch-rod.

For some delinquency now forgotten, Thomas had to undergo this terrible infliction. It nearly broke his heart. It is doubtful if any occurrence in after-life touched him so keenly. On returning home from school the woeful solemnity of his countenance indicated the anguish within. Tears, from a child upward, he never shed. It seemed he could not. For days in silent melancholy he brooded over his disgrace, as if his life were blasted. The incident made a lasting impression on his mind; never after did either schoolmistress or master find occasion for correction or reproof. He continued in Miss Stimson's

10

classes until the district or grammar school was opened. This higher educational institution was preceded by a school taught by Mr. Peter Vanevery, in the upper room of the first wooden court-house built in London. It stood between the site of the present court-house and the Robinson Hall. Mr. Vanevery was succeeded by Mr. Robertson, an Englishman, who complained that so long as he taught school for nothing, he was a good fellow; but when he asked for pay, every fault was found. On leaving, he wrote an article printed in the London *Sun*, first newspaper published in London, bitterly complaining of the way the people had treated him. The old wooden court-house was removed to the southwest corner of the square.

The first teacher of the new institution was Mr. John Talbot, who was succeeded by Mr. Boyce, and the latter by Mr. Francis H. Wright, M. A., a fine classical scholar. Mr. Boyce was an engineer by profession. After leaving the grammar school he was engaged by a few of the spirited citizens to survey the river Thames from London to its mouth, with a view of connecting the then village with the outside world by canal. Whether the report was favorable or adverse to the project, we are not aware. The incident is mentioned to show the enterprise of the infant forest city at that early date.

Thomas remained at the grammar school making rapid progress, until late in the year 1835. It was an excellent academy, and well attended. London was growing in houses, stores and population fast. Each additional family brought fresh numbers to augment the classes; the older and most advanced entering the higher establishment; the younger filling the school-room of Miss Stimson.

Among the earliest scholars at the grammar school, now remembered, besides Thomas Scatcherd, were: E. J. Parke, Thomas Parke, and their sister; John Scatcherd; James N. Scatcherd; George Schofield; Oliver Trow-bridge; James McFadden; Thomas Robertson; Hugh and Edward Richardson; R. Rapelgie; Sextus Kent; Thos. B. Rob; Geo. Darling; John and Edward Harris and two sisters; Henry Askin and two sisters; Henry Hamilton; John and Richard Stevens; Edward and Ralph Lee; D. J. Hughes (now County Court Judge of Elgin); Thomas and Verschoyle Cronyn and sister; Hiram Chisholm; John Terry; Robert Fennell and sister; Charles Kent; Charles and Thomas Travers; Charles and William K. Cornish; Charles Askin; Charles Duncombe, son of the late Dr. Duncombe of Burford Plains.

Many of those scholars are now dead, and others dispersed into different parts of the world.

Should this page meet the eye of any still living, they will doubtless recall the three sides of an oblong square marked on the floor with white chalk; up to which the scholars, when in class, were compelled to toe; the

teacher standing in the center. The instrument of punishment will also be remembered; a rope half an inch in
diameter, which the teacher doubled and kept continually
twisting. The cruel advantage taken of bare feet when a
word was missed or mistake made, cannot be forgotten;
nor can the lively skipping and jumping to avoid the
descending rope. Some were so active it required a number of trials to get in a satisfactory welt. To all who
were without shoes, and they were the majority, that was
a much-dreaded chalk mark.

There are those now living who have excellent reasons
for remembering a court, held by the scholars, with the
pupil D. J. Hughes as judge. The first step of the pros-
ecution in this mimic assize was to catch the prisoner,
who, having due notice, made the most of leg-bail. Escape, however, was impossible, for the whole court—judge,
jury, lawyers and spectators—assisted in running down
and arresting the alleged offender. They brought him
into court, where he was arraigned and assigned
counsel; a jury impaneled and witnesses examined.
The lawyers on each side accused and defended; the
judge summed up, and the jury gave a verdict of guilty;
no other verdict was rendered in that court. Then came
the sentence, quickly followed by the penalty.

There are those, too, who will remember that the late
Reverend Benjamin Cronyn, afterward Bishop of Huron,
resided in those days just across the street from the

school, and that he owned a large black-and-tan fox hound called "Sawney." Many of the boys brought their lunch to school, and it did seem as if there was no possible way of keeping the lunch from "Sawney," except by prematurely eating it. Just so sure as the hound saw it, the owner would eat no lunch that day. The dog continued to fill his lank sides until one day he took a luncheon specially prepared for him. This was his last; and the end of old "Sawney."

In 1836 there was tuition in the first log school-house, some two and a-half miles distant from Wyton; but Thomas did not attend it. Nearly five years at school in London left but little for him to learn in the rural log-house, though taught by the best country teacher then attainable. During the winter of 1837–38 he attended a school in London, on the corner of King and Talbot streets, taught by an old gentleman named Taylor; grandfather of John Taylor, Esq., barrister of London.

In the spring of 1838 Thomas Scatcherd returned to Wyton. On the farm he was incessant in his toil. His energy and industry were remarkable; never satisfied unless at work. At the plow and with the cradle he excelled; and in their use stood second to no young farmer of his own age in the neighborhood.

Hunting, fishing, shooting and other boyish sports possessed no attractions for him. He was passionately fond of books. Any one wishing to see Thomas was sure of finding him at work in the field, or in the house with a book.

In his fourteenth year, the young gentleman took a journey alone to Hamilton, eighty miles, with a team, and brought up a load of goods. This was considered a wonderful feat, as well as a daring adventure, by all who knew it—except himself. He did not highly estimate his own doings at any time.

During the next two years frequent trips were made to Hamilton, which largely increased his acquaintance, and gave him a little insight into life outside of a farm.

In his seventeenth year ambition for some calling different from a farmer's life manifested itself by the expression of a desire to obtain a profession. Fixing upon law for his future career, arrangements were made for gratifying this desire.

The life of the farmer during this year was exchanged for that of the student; and never did scholar more assiduously apply himself. He returned to the grammar school, still taught by Mr. Wright, but who was shortly afterwards succeeded by the Reverend Benjamin Bayly, M. A., under whom Thomas continued to pursue his studies, until he finally left school in 1842.

A new experience was about to open upon the boy, who was now suddenly required to appear before an august body of legal dignitaries, the barristers and judges who composed the benchers of the Law Society of Osgoode Hall, Toronto.

In the month of November, 1842, he passed the necessary examination before the benchers and was enrolled a member of the Law Society.

Returning to London, Mr. Scatcherd entered the law office of William Horton, Esq., and commenced his course of legal studies.

In the life of a law student there can be little worthy of placing on record. Mr. Horton's office was on the second flat of the Robinson Hall, near the east end on Dundas street, from whence he removed a year or two afterwards to the rooms in the court-house, now occupied as the sheriff's office.

The same desk can still be seen in Mr. Horton's office, just as it was when the young law student first took possession of it over thirty years ago; and at which he sat for the period of four years and four months.

In the fall of 1843 Mr. Scatcherd, then in his twentieth year, was sent by Mr. Horton to transact some business with the Hon. Colonel Talbot, at his residence on the shore of Lake Erie, in the township of Dunwich.

To those who have not had the honor of an acquaintance with the Colonel, it may be necessary to state that it required about as much courage for a youth and a stranger to call upon him on business as to face a battery.

Upon arriving at the Colonel's residence and finding

him engaged, Thomas sat down upon a log at a little distance from the house and awaited his leisure. Soon the
Colonel came up and accosted him with the question :
"What do you want?" interlarding his question with
expletives more forcible than polite. The youth commenced to explain his business, when he was cut short by
Talbot, who asseverated that all lawyers were a set of
rascals, and ordered the visitor off; telling him he would
do nothing for him. Young Scatcherd, however, was
firm and self-possessed ; and answered respectfully that
he would not go back without transacting the business
he had come about. Upon this Colonel Talbot called
him in, saying he was a manly fellow, and at once did the
business; and inquiring the name said he knew and had
a great respect for his father; offered a glass of wine,
and sent him away with as many pears as he could carry.

The above incident is mentioned to remark farther that
one of the secrets of Thomas Scatcherd's success in life
was his perfect coolness under trying circumstances, and
determination not to be diverted from the performance of
duty, no matter what obstacles lay in his path.

In January, 1845, but little more than two years after
he had commenced his studies, he had become acquainted
with the leading men of London. Reference to books of
the corporation shows that he was in that month appointed Clerk of the Board of Police; the duties of which
office he performed in a highly satisfactory manner,

exercising the same care and attention in the discharge of civic service as in the performance of every duty, public or private, that he was called upon to fulfill in after-life.

The duties which he performed during this year were by no means light. The great fire which broke out in the Robinson Hall swept away nearly the whole of the business part of the town, and prepared the way for new duties and labors on the part of the corporation of an exceptional character; and consequently threw a vast amount of additional work upon the clerk which required both skill and ability to accomplish. But with a perseverance and industry which would have done credit to a man of mature years, he was enabled to perform the duties of his office in a highly efficient manner.

The best evidence of the confidence reposed in him, for the fidelity with which he discharged his duty as clerk of the board is the fact that, when the new council was elected in the following year, consisting, with one exception, of different men, he was again unanimously chosen to perform the same services of clerk; which office he continued to fill with equal satisfaction to the board and to the public.

Mr. Scatcherd wishing to pursue his studies in Toronto, requested the board to select his fellow-student, the late Henry Hamilton, in his stead. This gentleman was son of the late James Hamilton, Esq., Sheriff of Middlesex. In February, 1844, he entered Mr. Horton's office, and in due time was called to the Bar and practiced his profession. A warm and lasting friendship sprang up between the fellow-students. While still in that office Mr. Scatcherd, by his steady habits and the implicit confidence reposed in him by the public, secured a large amount of business in the way of the collection of small accounts, and in Division Court matters; and from the business habits thus acquired he laid the foundation of his future success.

In the spring of 1847 he left the office of Mr. Horton and finished his studies with the Messrs. Duggan, barristers in Toronto.

Mr. Scatcherd was called to the Bar in Hilary term, February, 1848, and immediately commenced the practice of his profession in London. There a partnership was formed with his intimate friend and old school-fellow, E. Jones Parke, Esq., who managed the business of the law firm at the town of Woodstock, county of Oxford. This copartnership lasted until the year 1852. It was then dissolved and Mr. Parke returned to London.

Mr. Parke was son of the late Hon. Thomas Parke, who, after the Union, was appointed to the ministry as Surveyor-General of Canada; which office he held until it was abolished in 1844.

The long period of thirty years has now elapsed (1878) since Mr. Scatcherd was called to the Bar. To those whose memory does not extend so far back, and to those 'only it is necessary to say that he at once took a high position. His well-known honest, straightforward character combined with industrious business habits, together with his great abilities and sound judgment, brought him friends from all quarters; and the result was that he secured a leading and respectable business in his profession.

As a speaker at the Bar he displayed an earnestness and candor of expression which invariably had great weight with the jury. And although he made no pretension to the display of florid oratory, nor to any of those clap-trap tricks which are occasionally practised for the purpose of influencing a jury, he at times, when laboring under a deep sense of wrong inflicted upon his client, spoke with an eloquence and force rarely exceeded by any of his professional brethren.

Always cautious in advising a resort to litigation, he rarely became engaged in a cause in which he did not feel certain of success; and the result was that he very seldom lost a case before a jury, except when clients insisted on litigation contrary to his advice.

He detested fraud or wrong of any kind; and when he had occasion to denounce them, brought to his aid powers of invective, sarcasm and wit, under which the unfortunate delinquent was made to feel that the way of the transgressor is hard; and that honesty is the best policy. Every one who has habitually attended our courts of justice, has witnessed the difficulty of eliciting truth from an unwilling witness; and the evasions to which witnesses resort to favor the party in whose interest they are swearing. Mr. Scatcherd in the course of his practice had many an encounter with characters of this sort, and generally succeeded in compelling them to tell the whole truth.

He possessed an excellent knowledge of human character; was an exceedingly close observer; and being intimately acquainted not only with the habits and mode of thinking among the jury, but well understood the business of their every-day life, he knew precisely what chord to strike in order to excite their sympathies. He thus enlisted their feelings in favor of his client to a degree altogether unattainable by an advocate less accustomed to study mankind.

During the commercial crisis of 1856, which involved thousands of persons in difficulty and some in ruin, so great was the confidence reposed in Mr. Scatcherd by business men, that his services were in constant demand either in assisting to wind up estates, or in the securing and collecting of debts. His time was wholly occupied, and the weight of business thrown upon his hands would have been a strain upon the mind of any man. But by perseverance, and untiring industry, he found himself equal to the occasion; and so far as we have heard, performed his work to the entire satisfaction of all parties.

A difficult task indeed, when the conflicting and adverse interests which he had to contend with are considered.

Of all the important cases in which Mr. Scatcherd was concerned, perhaps there was not one, the result of which afforded him more unmixed satisfaction and just pride, than the celebrated action brought some ten years ago by McDonough & Kent, against several insurance companies.

This firm, then carrying on an extensive mercantile business in London, had their stock and property destroyed by fire; having at the time a large insurance on their goods. This insurance the companies refused to pay, on the ground that the value of goods destroyed was greatly over-estimated. Several actions were instituted against the companies. Some of the most distinguished members of the Bar of Ontario were engaged. The battle was fought out to the end, extending over several days, and resulted in verdicts amounting to over thirty thousand dollars against the companies.

Mr. Scatcherd, as solicitor for the plaintiffs, felt that most of the responsibility of preparing the cases, looking over the pleadings, and having the facts fairly laid before the different juries, devolved upon him.

When we consider the technical difficulties attending actions such as these, and the manner in which the insurance companies are protected by conditions and rules, applicable to no other corporate bodies, railways only excepted; and that however just a claim may be, or no matter what the loss a party may have sustained, he is liable, at any moment during the progress of the trial, to have his claim thrown out of court and himself deprived of the fruits of his insurance: And, if he fail in proving that immediately after the fire he gave the proper notice of his loss, and made affidavit how the fire originated—or, if he otherwise neglected to comply with the many conditions with which these companies are hedged in, the case may be lost: And further that, after all has been done by the assured and every condition complied with he may still fail to recover, unless he has a host of witnesses on hand at the right time to prove the conditions have been fulfilled. Such being the contingencies, the fact is realized that all these matters, requiring to be looked sharply after, subjected Mr. Scatcherd to many anxious thoughts during the protracted trial of those important suits.

When the trials were over and the victory won, the whole party—plaintiffs, attorneys and counsel engaged on their behalf—sat together for their photographs; copies of which were distributed amongst them, and will long remain in their families, as mementoes of one of the most important events in the legal history of the county.

On the 25th of June, 1851, Mr. Scatcherd married Isabella Sprague, an exceedingly amiable young lady, daughter of the late Thomas Sprague, Esquire, of the township of Yarmouth, in the county of Elgin, and grand-daughter of the late Elias Moore, Esquire, M. P. for the county of Middlesex, in the Parliament of Upper Canada, previous to the Union of 1841.

Early in the career of Mr. Scatcherd, he received the appointment of City Solicitor, a position held until his death. The duties of this office are sometimes difficult, and always important, involving the advising upon and framing of by-laws, on all sorts of matters; the construction to be placed upon the various and often conflicting sections of Acts of Parliament; the drafting and examination of covenants and deeds affecting the corporation; the defending of actions brought against that body; and many other things, requiring the greatest care and the strictest attention.

In the year 1861 Mr. Scatcherd took as law partner his former pupil, Mr. William Ralph Meredith, present member of the Ontario Legislature for the city of London. In all matters connected with business, the strictest confidence and most friendly relations existed between them.

Mr. Scatcherd was practically generous, but did good in secret, not allowing his left hand to know what the right hand did. No apology need be made for giving publicity to his characteristic mode of doing kindness in the following instance, as it has already been referred to in the public press: One of the most worthy citizens of London, many years ago, was threatened with the loss of a valuable office under the corporation, unless he could immediately raise $1,200 to pay off a supposed deficiency caused in adding up an account. He told his trouble to Mr. Scatcherd, who was at the time engaged writing, and who expressed sorrow for him, but could not see any way out of the trouble, and feared the position would be lost. The gentleman got up to retire almost heart-broken, when the barrister, handing him a letter, said, "My clerks are out; will you be kind enough to hand this to the teller of the bank, and ask him if the contents are right?" Upon the letter being handed to the teller, he asked the gentleman how he would have his money. The letter contained Mr. Scatcherd's check for $1,200. This was the act of a Christian; equal, so far as example goes, to the work of the Good Samaritan. It was in practical harmony with the Sermon on the Mount. Many other acts of kindness and benevolence, always performed by stealth, have accidently come to our knowledge. A mere verbal sympathy was not given. He appeared to know nothing of that way of assisting others, or expressing his own feelings. As some trouble or necessity was related, his lips became thinner, the face and features more pale and cold. As you proceeded with a statement of wants, specifying the extent of aid desired, an impression came that the application was a failure, and words were being wasted on a cold, apathetic listener; but, in this momentary despondency, you would receive sympathy so substantial as not helped merely a little, but completely ended the trouble. And this would be done in such manner as to leave no opportunity for returning thanks. The act was ended and the gentleman out of sight before you were aware of what he had done.

> "Careless their merits, or their wants to scan,
> His pity gave ere charity began."

Instances of impulse, with an affinity to the sentiment of those lines, have been related by associates. One or two, though inconsiderable in degree, may be re-told here as personal characteristics of the man.

In New Orleans, Mr. Scatcherd stood with a friend one day on the levee. They were a few feet, apart when he was approached by an Italian orange-vender, who, with beseeching eyes, said, "Buy orange?" Looking for a moment at her tattered clothes and weary face, he said, "How much?" Her reply was, "Two, twenty-five cent." He took from his pocket a silver twenty-five-cent piece," holding it in view in one hand, while with the other he began turning the oranges over, digging down to the bottom of the basket. Her eyes caught sight of the coin and glistened as she viewed it. The premium then made the currency value of it fifty cents. "Perhaps the stranger may give me that for two oranges," was the anxious expression of her features. On raising her eyes and noticing the cold and hardening expression of the

11

customer's face, as he continued to turn the fruit over and
over, her countenance fell.　Taking another look at him,
she evidently gave up hope of his taking even one orange,
and began hitching away, her face crimson and eyes
flashing with indignation.　Just before it was too late
he took two oranges, handed her the silver piece, and
returned the fruit to the basket with a smile so sweetly
filled with kindness it seemed to reach and warm her
heart.　Quick as a flash the woman took in the situation,
and moved to thank him; but too late, he was walking away.　She looked after him a moment or two as if
wishing he might turn around, but he did not.　She
laid her basket down and gazed, as if expecting the
by-standers must have noticed the transaction, and then
resumed her business.　As he was walking next day with
his friend, they met the woman.　The bow with which
she expressed recognition and remembrance of the occurrence, was as graceful as his embarrassment was con-
fusing.　He remarked to his friend, "That woman thinks
she must have seen you before."

Mr. Scatcherd remained over night at a hotel in a
small village, where his profession frequently called
him.　On one occasion having no smaller money than
a twenty-dollar gold-piece, he handed it to the landlord
in settling his bill.　Unable to make the change, the
landlord returned the money, saying: "You can make
it right the first time I am in London."

The hostler, hearing the conversation, volunteered to make change. The offer was accepted. Disappearing for a few minutes, he returned with a small bag containing twenty dollars in silver, all fifty-cent pieces.

After Mr. Scatcherd left, the landlord, curious to know where his hostler got so much money, asked the question, and received this reply: "I got every piece of it from Mr. Scatcherd; he never stopped here without giving me a fifty-cent piece. I can tell by the number I have, he has been here just forty times since I came to work for you."

Although Mr. Scatcherd had not yet "fallen into the sere and yellow leaf," he had long acquired in an eminent degree "that which should accompany old age—honor, love, obedience, troops of friends." He seldom lost a client or a friend; and indeed it was impossible he could do so, as his kind and obliging manners endeared him to every one with whom he came in contact.

We are aware that during the time of the great depression in the country—1856-'57—to which reference has already been made, he frequently indorsed heavily for his friends and clients; and indeed for many others who had little or no claim upon him, and thus saved them from bankruptcy or ruin. But owing to his sound judgment and foresight, he did not lose largely as the result of his kindness; although, no doubt, the liabilities incurred in this way often caused anxiety and trouble.

Had it not been for his large and lucrative practice, he would, from good nature, have suffered serious embarrassment at times.

Before dismissing this part of the Memoir, the learned gentleman's personal appearance may be described. He was of medium height, standing about five feet nine inches, with broad shoulders and strong muscular frame. Rather stout in person than otherwise, but by no means corpulent. The head was unusually large, towering above the ears; the broad and massive brow indicating a very large brain, with great intellectual power and firmness. The eyes were gray. The hair brown and wavy; in his younger days exceedingly thick, but latterly thin. The complexion rather dark than fair. Quiet and sedate in all movements, he never appeared in a hurry. Having complete control of his emotions, and observing everything done by others, it was exceedingly difficult to penetrate the thoughts working in his mind. He cared little for general society, or for the gaiety and frivolities of large parties. With one or two intimate friends, when he could discuss professional or political matters and news of the day, or relate anecdotes affecting public and professional men, he greatly enjoyed himself. But knowing his affectionate disposition, and extreme fondness for his beloved wife and children, we feel assured that his greatest enjoyment was at his own fireside, in the society and companionship of those dear objects of his affections.

The death of Mr. Scatcherd's father in 1858 proved the signal for several candidates to assert their pretensions to the vacant seat in the Reform interest in West Middlesex. Amongst others, the Reverend William Wilkinson, Mr. James Daniell, and Mr. Archibald Campbell may be mentioned. Mr. Wilkinson was, however, chosen the standard-bearer to fight the battle, having for his opponent an old friend, A. P. McDonald, who had unsuccessfully opposed the lately-deceased member in the previous contest. Upon this occasion, Mr. McDonald was elected over Mr. Wilkinson, and held his seat until the general election of 1861.

This is, properly speaking, the commencement of the political career of the late Thomas Scatcherd. In 1861 he came for the first time before the public as a candidate for political honors. Recalling the fact that Mr. A. P. McDonald was a resident of the Riding, and was already the sitting member; a man of large means; undoubtedly popular; a supporter of the ministry and thoroughly versed in all the arts of managing an election, we realize that it required moral courage on the part of Mr. Scatcherd, an untried man and member of a profession which is generally supposed to be too strongly represented in the Legislature, to oppose such a man as Mr. McDonald. He was, moreover, opposed by the *Free*

Press and *Prototype* newspapers, and had no local city organ to support his claim.

On 10th of June, 1861, a Reform Convention was held at Strathroy, when the claims of several parties were freely discussed. It was, however, pretty well understood that Mr. Scatcherd would be the almost unanimous choice of that body, and upon a vote being taken, he stood 43 to 4. Mr. Scatcherd having thus proved the strongest man to fight the battle of Reform against his formidable opponent, threw himself into the contest. His friends went vigorously to work. Meetings were held throughout the Riding, and as thorough a canvass of the electors made as the space of time permitted. It was well known the contest would be a close one, and consequently extraordinary efforts were put forth by the friends of each contending party to insure the desired result.

At close of the poll the votes stood:

Scatcherd, ...	1532
McDonald, ...	1342
Majority for Scatcherd, ...	190

Having thus been elected by a handsome majority he took his seat in Parliament for the West Riding of Middlesex; which position was held until the general election of 1863. He voted and acted generally with the Reform party; and introduced a bill, having for its object the reduction of law costs. Although he failed to carry this measure, his earnest advocacy of the bill was appreciated, not only by his constituents, but by many outsiders. In connection with this the following is reproduced from the local press:

DESERVED COMPLIMENT.—A few of the admirers of Mr. Thomas Scatcherd, intend presenting that gentleman with a very handsome silver snuff-box, as a mark of their esteem and regard for him; more particularly in consequence of his commendable efforts in Parliament with reference to the Law Reform Bill, which he so ably advocated, and which, if successfully carried through, will prove very beneficial to the Province generally.

The inscription on the snuff-box is as follows:

PRESENTED TO THOMAS SCATCHERD, ESQUIRE, BY A FEW FRIENDS IN WESTMINSTER, C. W., AS A MARK OF RESPECT FOR HIS UPRIGHT CONDUCT IN PARLIAMENT. JUNE 4th, 1863.

The presentation was made by the late Charles Stewart, Esq., J. P.

Being a new member, modest and retiring in his nature and habits, he was not, at this early period of his career, a frequent speaker. Nor did he attempt to take a prominent part in the proceedings of the House; but applied himself earnestly as a member of committees. From his legal knowledge, sound judgment, and well-known ability, he was called upon to perform a large amount of committee work. Co-incidently, he became acquainted with the rules of the House, and the details of parliamentary routine; laying a sure foundation for the reputation afterwards acquired upon all points involving the rules and manner of procedure in the Legislature.

The writer of " Pen Pictures " in the *Hamilton Times* sent the following from Ottawa :

MR. SCATCHERD, M. P.—On the front row of opposition benches, next to the member for Halton, sits Mr. Scatcherd, member for North Middlesex. This gentleman is son of the late John Scatcherd, who sat for a number of years in the old Parliament of Canada, and who was a consistent supporter of reform measures. Mr. Scatcherd is a well-known barrister of the Forest City, and much esteemed professionally and otherwise. In appearance he does not look unlike an Episcopal clergyman. He is a good speaker, both in matter and in manner. His speeches are not very long, but they are to the point, and are couched in unexceptionable English. He is one of the comparatively few members who are listened to with pleasure, only speaks when he really has something to say, and when he says it stops."

In the summer of 1863 Parliament was again dissolved and writs for a general election forthwith issued. Mr. A. P. McDonald, who had been defeated by Mr. Scatcherd two years previously, declined another contest with his increasingly-popular antagonist ; but Mr. Thomas Moyle, a local man, residing in the township of Metcalfe, resolved upon entering the lists. This gentleman had been Reeve of his township, and being a man of excellent character, education and ability, he reasonably expected that his claim upon the Riding might meet with success. But the result proved he had miscalculated the public feeling. Every effort was made to destroy Mr. Scatcherd's popularity, by attempting to prove that as Solicitor for the City of London, he had been party to an arbitration, injuriously affecting the interests of the county ; a charge which so far as he was concerned had no foundation whatever, and which was promptly confuted at the time.

Notwithstanding all the benefit which Mr. Moyle's friends derived from the circulation of this and other reports intended to prejudice his opponent's interests in the Riding, Mr. Scatcherd, at close of the poll, was declared duly elected. The vote stood :

Scatcherd, ...	1626
Moyle, ...	548
Majority for Scatcherd, ...	1078

On the day of declaration, after the Returning Officer declared Mr. Scatcherd duly elected by this decisive majority, the member thanked the people for his return as their representative a second time. He attributed the result to his course in Parliament. He was gratified by the large majority. He had been opposed on party principles, but had relied on the constituency for an approving decision, on the ground of having fulfilled in Parliament the pledges given at the previous election, namely : To judge bills introduced by Government, or by the opposition, on their merits ; and on those merits vote for or vote against them. If he could not discern right from wrong, irrespective of parties, his presence would be useless in the Legislature.

They had decided that the course pursued was alike
honorable and useful.

He thanked his friends in all the municipalities for
their support, and in taking leave hoped if he came again
before them it would be with as clean hands as at this
time.

Thus, in the space of two years from his first entrance
into public life, the Member for Middlesex had been
borne on the tide to the highest wave of popular favor.
He had succeded in crushing out successful opposition in
his constituency; and, owing to the honest, straightforward and moderate course pursued by him in Parliament,
was almost equally approved and trusted by both sides of
the House. He now applied himself vigorously to his
public duties; took part in the debates, and was listened
to with the greatest respect His character became
better known in the House; and he was frequently
appointed chairman of committees. In this position his
judicial mind and well-known impartiality insured justice
and fair-play to all parties.

Canada was fast reaching an important point in her
political history. The party in power—Conservative—
had not an efficient working majority. The opposition
was strong enough when party lines were strictly drawn
to greatly impede, if not obstruct, legislation, but too
weak to carry a vote of want of confidence. Business in
Parliament was at a dead-lock. The exciting question of

Representation by Population had been agitated by the people for years, and was then pressing on the Legislature for settlement.

The British Colonies in North America, extending from the Atlantic to the Pacific ocean, divided only by ideal lines, each Province with a separate Legislature, had little interest in common except loyalty to the mother country. Thoughtful minds of both parties viewed the political condition of Canada with extreme anxiety. A confederation of the Provinces seemed a remedy for the present, and was likely to insure prosperity and greatness in the future. Neither political party being strong enough to carry such a measure, some of the ablest men from both sides, and representative men from the different Provinces, united and held a convention at the city of Quebec, in October, 1864. The idea of confederation was freely discussed and the main principle approved.

In the parliamentary session of 1866, Sir John Macdonald, Attorney-General and leader of the House, moved :

" That a humble address be presented to Her Majesty, praying that she may be graciously pleased to cause a measure to be submitted to the Imperial Parliament, for the purpose of uniting the Colonies of Canada, Nova Scotia, New Brunswick, Newfoundland and Prince Edward Island, in one Government; with provisions based on certain resolutions, which were adopted at a conference of delegates from the said Colonies, held at the city of Quebec, on the tenth of October, 1864."

As might be expected, there was diversity of opinion among the members, irrespective of party, on this great question; and a lively debate followed, lasting considerably over a month.

The debate was more than lively. It was characterized by an out-flow of patriotic utterances from Canadian statesmen, diverse in race, language, religion, politics and social sympathies; but in one sentiment all agreeing, namely—to build up an enduring common country on principles harmonizing with the Imperial parent nations in Europe, and with the illustrious companion people in America.

On the seventh of March Mr. Scatcherd addressed the House. The position taken by the learned member was judicial rather than political. He was not opposed to the principle of union in itself; but questioned the inter-provincial justice of the scheme in some of the parts, which imposed for a future time financial responsibilities of perilous amount, and redistributed the public debt unequally. The philosophic student of history will read [in the officially reported debates of 1865] the speech of Mr. Scatcherd in the light of the circumstances then impelling political party leaders to seek constitutional experiments. In its study, now at the distance of thirteen years, the mental powers of the man continue to come out before the intellectual reader with the reality of a personal presence. The speech was history, prophecy, current statistics, conflicting political circumstances, philosophically blended and unfolded on floor of the House of Parliament by a statesman of judicial mind, who was great because able and earnest; who knew he was earnest; hardly knew he was able; did not know he was great.

CHAPTER IX.

Mr. Thomas Scatcherd, M. P.

ON the first of July, 1867, the Act of Confederation came into operation and a new nationality was conferred upon the people. Parliament expired by lapse of time, and a general election became necessary. In accordance with the Union Act, an increased representation was granted to Ontario. The West Riding of Middlesex, hitherto represented by Mr. Scatcherd, was divided. By adding to the Northern portion the townships of Biddulph, and McGillivray taken from the county of Huron, a new Division was formed, called the North Riding of Middlesex; comprising the townships of Adelaide, Lobo, Biddulph, McGillivray, East and West Williams.

About the first of September, writs were issued for a general election; and Mr. Scatcherd, having been urged by influential parties in the new riding to take the field, consented. A convention was held at the village of Ailsa Craig, when the names of several prominent gentlemen were brought forward for nomination in the Reform interest. Mr. Scatcherd, being called upon, made a speech, characterized by a high-toned and independent exposition of his past career, and of his intended future course, should they think proper to give him the nomination.

" He did not engage that, in running for the Legislature, he was to be tied fast to any political party, bound to follow it through thick and thin. Nor would he undertake, if returned, to support any particular Government."

This is different from the style of address heard from political adventurers, who, for the sake of parliamentary honors suffer themselves to be blindly led to oppose everything, good or bad, which does not emanate from the party with which they are, for the time, in general accord.

The delegates then proceeded to select their candidate, with the following result :

Scatcherd, ... 25
G. W. Ross (Lobo), ... 13
H. M. Wilkinson (Widder), ... 10

Having obtained a majority of the votes of all the delegates present, Mr. Scatcherd was declared the nominee of the convention for the new House of Commons.

Mr. William Watson was nominated standard-bearer for the Conservative party. He was long and favorably known as a resident of the riding, and being a farmer, and Highland Scotchman of good education and plausi-

ble manners, his party, and indeed his opponents, felt
that he was no mean antagonist.

The election took place about the 20th day of Septem-
• ber, when the following proved to be the result:

Scatcherd, ...	1602
Watson, ...	871
Majority for Scatcherd, ...	731

This majority was larger than Mr. Scatcherd or his
friends anticipated. It certainly was a surprise to Mr.
Watson and his friends; and proved how firmly the member elect was seated in the confidence and affections of
the people.

He had now been returned three times to Parliament;
and in proportion as he gained ground in the esteem of
his constituents, he likewise acquired the respect and
regard of his fellow-members of both parties.

He had become an experienced member of the Legislature, and exercised an influence in the House justly due
to his popularity in the country, as well as to an extensive knowledge of parliamentary law, and his independent character.

Mr. Scatcherd's duties on committee during the day,
and in attending and taking part in the debates at night,
engrossed his whole time. Whatever his doubts and
misgivings may have been, as to the effect of the act
constituting the Federal Union, he now felt that it be-

came every lover of his country to assist the Government
of the day, in rearing and consolidating that fabric, the
foundation of which had only been laid. He knew that
to succeed in that great undertaking, the Government
required the assistance and encouragement of the people ;
and he felt that it would be unpatriotic and unjust to
thwart the party in power in their attempt to complete
their work. He felt that it was a time when a public
man, entrusted by the people with their interests, should
rise superior to party, and act solely for the welfare of the
country, in its attempt to enlarge its confines and emerge
into a nation. Mr. Scatcherd occasionally voted with the
Government, and against his party, when feeling, that
by so doing, he was best serving the interests of his
country.

The Hon. Sir Francis Hincks had been a life-long
Reformer ; and, as such, possessed the confidence of the
Reform party. Upon his retirement from the government of British Guiana, being prevailed upon by Sir
John Macdonald to assume the office of Finance Minister, it was well known that the office had fallen into the
hands of a man of consummate ability in that particular
department, however much the party-men may have dis-
agreed as to the propriety of his joining a conservative
government.

The leaders of the opposition looked upon him as little
better than a turn-coat and a traitor, who had deserted

12

his old Reform principles, and were not disposed to give him that measure of fair-play to which he was entitled in the trying task of harmonizing and reducing into system and order the financial affairs of five different provinces.

Mr. Scatcherd was, however, not among those who desired to throw obstacles in the way of this eminent minister; and, when Sir Francis introduced his Bank of Issue scheme, the Member for North Middlesex warmly supported the measure on the ground, as he himself alleged, that "The Bank of Upper Canada having failed, some such measure was requisite to prevent a repetition of that ruin."

The leaders of the opposition, with whom he was identified as a Reformer, were not well satisfied with the vote on this occasion, as they had strong hopes of defeating the Government on this or some kindred measure. An under-current of disapproval in regard to this and some other votes, which he felt it his duty to give, in support of the measures of the party in power, had crept into parts of his constituency, and covert threats were made that a more advanced Reformer would be brought forward to contest the riding at the next general election.

It was even alleged, we know not whether truly or not, that orders had been issued in high quarters, that he was to be opposed at all hazards, as not sufficiently in accord with the policy of his leaders, which policy was to over-

turn the government of Sir John Macdonald as speedily
as possible, and seize the reins of power.

It is true that he had always been a Reformer, as his
father was before him.   It is true that he had, for twelve
years, ably represented West and North Middlesex in
Parliament, after having overcome his Tory opponents in
three fiercely-contested elections.   It is also true that in
1867 he had been elected by the Reform party by an
overwhelming majority, after he had declared his intention of giving the Government of Sir John a fair trial.
Yet, notwithstanding all this, the more violent party-men
among his former supporters, considered that the only
fair trial to be given the ministry was to oppose them on
all questions and on every occasion, and to defeat them
on the first opportunity.   Mr. Scatcherd could not share
in that kind of opposition.   He felt that duty to himself,
as well as to his country and to his constituents, was to
judge measures on their merits, and to aid ministers, as
far as he consistently could, in completing the great work
of confederation then going on.   Such was the political
philosophy and legislative patriotism of the learned member in relation to the ministry, the opposition and the
country.

A member of the House of Commons says: " When
I went to Parliament, Mr. Scatcherd was considered one
of the old members.   The seat assigned me was on his
left, just across a narrow alley.   We sat there two ses-

sions without either speaking to the other. During a
third session, I inquired of a member, 'What manner of
a man is that Scatcherd?' and related the kind of neighbors we had been, remarking that on account of my being
a younger member, I naturally expected the first ad-
vances would come from him. He said, 'My friend, you
don't know him. I tell you he is one of the most obliging men in the House, when you understand him. The
first time you feel in need of any assistance just go right
to him, the same as if you had known him all your life,
and tell him what you want.' A few days after, I wished
to present a resolution of some importance; and, feeling
I needed advice and assistance, went to Mr. Scatcherd
and told him. He took the papers from my hand, drew
the resolution, giving all the information I required; and,
without adding a single outside word about anything,
returned me the papers. The way in which this little kindness was done, expressed the pleasure he felt in doing it.
I saw plainly I did not understand the man, and thereafter learned to appreciate and esteem him. From that
time to his death a warm friendship existed between us.
I think he rarely lost a friend after making one; but,
as a rule, he very seldom did the making."

In 1872 Parliament expired by lapse of time, and writs
were issued for a general election. A convention was
held at Ailsa Craig, for the purpose of bringing out a
candidate for the North Riding of Middlesex, which had

been represented by Mr. Scatcherd since 1867. The convention system has now become a fixed institution in the country, and on the whole works well, but it is not always a reflex of popular feeling. In the present instance, the Lobo delegates, in casting their votes against the previous member, represented no more than the choice of a minority of the Reform votes of that township. In other words, the delegation for that township was got up in the interest of a person supposed to be more in harmony with the extreme views of some of the party.

However this may be, Mr. Scatcherd was not the sort of man to be diverted from the course he had marked out for himself, no matter whether they chose to nominate him or not.

The name of Mr. John Waters, a highly respectable farmer of East Williams, who had held the office of Reeve of that township, and has since been chosen Warden of the county, was brought before the convention by the party opposed to Mr. Scatcherd; and now the test was to be made as to which of these gentlemen would be the nominee of this convention. Mr. Scatcherd was first called upon to address that body, and in a long . and earnest address, occupying over two hours, he fully explained his parliamentary action. A writer has said of him at this time :

" When we consider the peculiar position in which he was placed, with a probable opponent to contend against in the Conservative interest, and a division in the Reform ranks, we are justified in saying that his speech on this occasion was characterized by a bold, fearless and manly exposition of his political principles, almost amounting to rashness, evincing as it did that, however much he valued his seat and position in Parliament, he was willing to relinquish both one and the other, rather than submit to the dictation of party at the expense of principle. No doubt Mr. Scatcherd felt hurt and indignant that, after all his labors in the interests of Reform, an attempt should now be made by a wing of the party to cast him aside, and supplant him by a candidate less independent."

The result proved, however, that he was as deep in the confidence and affections of the great body of the people as ever, for when the vote was taken, it stood:

Scatcherd, ... 48
Waters, ... 19
Majority for Scatcherd, ... 29

The following is a summary of Mr. Scatcherd's speech, delivered before the Convention voted. It was reported in the Park Hill *Gazette*, which warmly advocated the interest of its friend, Mr. Waters:

Speech of Mr. T. Scatcherd to the Convention held at Ailsa Craig, July, 1872.

He said he came before them at this time in no way changed in principles or practice from the time he had last appeared before this convention. He had represented North Middlesex for the last five years, and had before that represented the then united constituencies of North and West Middlesex. Altogether he had been a representative of this county for about twelve years, and felt that he had reason to be proud of his position and the continuance of public confidence expressed in him. In viewing his votes and his conduct for the term which he had represented them, he felt there was nothing to repent of; and there was not one vote that he had given, but he would repeat, were he placed in the same position again. All he had to say to this convention was, that if elected by them (and he would not run unless accepted by the convention) and accepted by the constituency, he would continue to act as he always had done.

Five years ago when he last appeared to contest the election in this riding in the interests of Reform, there were very few Reformers who could be induced to offer themselves to the constituency. To elect a Reformer at that time was no easy matter. He had won back the constituency from the hands of the Conservatives to its proper position as a Reform constituency. Since he had been in Parliament some of his friends had called him in question for not voting strictly with his party; but those friends and this convention would remember that he had promised a "fair trial" policy if returned, and that after being elected on such a vote, and after making such promises, it would have been unmanly and indecent in him to have turned round and fiercely opposed the Government until they had had an opportunity to explain their policy. In abstaining from a factious opposition, he was prepared to justify in detail every vote given. He had no promises to make that he would do better than he had done;

but was prepared to meet any one who objected to his votes at every school-house in the riding, and there defend his votes, and leave it to the electors to judge whether he had been right or wrong.

He had never aspired for any office under Government; nor had he ever received one. He did not represent this constituency for any object of personal aggrandisement, but was proud of his position as representative of such a constituency, and laboring for their good and our country's, was his sole object and aim. He acknowledged that some of his votes were not strictly party ones. He believed that many old issues between Conservatives and Reformers were dead, and should not be revived. He instanced the weakness of the Reform party in the country, and asked what was the use in such a weak party endeavoring to oust a Government which was in such a majority. It would have been a fruitless struggle; and he considered he was doing better by accepting every measure on its merits. He acknowledged that he had voted with the Government—every member in the House had done the same thing. He voted for the measures, and not for the Government; and considered that his single vote was of no account, even had he voted against the Government and against their preponderating majorities. He had not deserted the party in 1864 for a coalition. His opinions about confederation were expressed at last election, and were indorsed by this constituency. He had therefore nothing to urge on that subject, further than that his opinions then, were his opinions now.

All this clamor about Reform and Conservatism in Ontario amounts to very little in the Dominion Parliament. There were convened members from Nova Scotia and New Brunswick who knew nothing about the principles of the two parties. There was no such parties in those two provinces; with them it was—support the Government which would do the most for them. In detailing the Government majorities from each province, he explained that it was useless to suppose, that the present opposition could get into or remain in power, except they were willing to truckle to those provinces, which had no politics but that of their own aggrandizement. These would support any Government which favored them, and it was useless for Reformers to expect success in the Dominion Parliament while they held to their present extreme principles. After giving his views anent the Nova Scotia subsidy, and the evil results arising therefrom, he again recurred to his own votes and defied the finger of envy or scorn to point to one vote which he had given that was prompted by selfishness. He advised the convention to be careful of their position. They should endeavor to prevent anything like a division. In the cry that he had done nothing for his riding, there was neither sense nor reason. This county was an agricultural one, and it was impossible to legislate for the benefit of the country as a whole without benefiting Middlesex; and there was no opportunity or necessity for special legislation in our behalf.

He then went on to speak of the different political parties, Reform and Conservative. He said that Reformers never made successful Governments, and instanced our own Government, from 1840 up to the present; also the Government of Gladstone, in England. Reformers, he said were too extreme in their views. They aimed at perfection, and the consequence was that they were governmental failures. Their utopianism did well for opposition, but so soon as they became the governing power, they at once saw the impossibility of carrying out their entire principles. If they persisted in legislating strictly according to their policy while in opposition, they were sure to be defeated by their opponents and the moderate men. If they forsook any of their previous platforms, their own friends would turn against them and they would lose the respect of all parties. Reformers professed too much—more·than they were able to fulfill. Gladstone was an instance of this. He went into power with a large majority, but on account of his persistant efforts for extreme reform legislation, he was now on the eve of defeat. In Canada we never had a single Reform leader of the Government, who did not become tabooed by his party in the end. He instanced Hincks, Baldwin, John S. McDonald, M. Cameron and many others, as once accepted Reformers, but who now were obliged to associate with the other party, simply because of the utopianism of Reform.

In the Reform party there was no single object but a conglomeration of advocates of different species of Reforms. These could never hold together, simply because of a dissimilarity of interests. The Conservative party is a unit. It has no divisions nor undeviable line of principle, and it therefore is wide enough to take in the disaffected of all parties and not quarrel with them. Hence its uniform strength. It seemed impossible for the Reformers, each one holding peculiar ideas of his own, and inflexibly insisting on them, to form a successful Government. Each member of a Government must understand that he is only one of perhaps a dozen, and that he must give and take, and bide his time for the accomplishment of his cherished one idea.

He said a man who manages a farm of one thousand acres, and employs twenty to thirty men; or a merchant of a similarly important enterprise, although highly successful in their avocations, would, in going to Parliament, find they could not control the House of Commons as they had done their own particular business. He did not consider himself a heaven-born orator, and it was beyond the power of one little man like himself to accomplish the overthrow of the present Government, however devoutly he might wish for such an event. He would, at any of the sessions after the first one of the last Parliament, have voted a want of confidence had it been proposed, but such a motion would have been entirely futile. Mr. Scatcherd then closed his speech by saying that on his past conduct the convention must judge him. He could promise nothing better.

Thus were extinguished the hopes of the malcontents; and Mr. Scatcherd, being now the only candidate in the field, was on the day of nomination at the general election in August, 1872, declared by the Returning Officer duly elected to represent the free and independent electors of the North Riding of Middlesex, without opposition.

The Conservatives refrained on this occasion from offering a futile opposition, by bringing forward a candidate; and, indeed, the independent course of Mr. Scatcherd in Parliament had, to a great extent, disarmed opposition in that quarter. The Conservatives knew he was not a follower of Sir John Macdonald, and that no worldly consideration would induce him to forsake those principles of reform which he had always professed. But they felt that he was thoroughly honest and conscientious in his votes, whether for or against the policy of the Government, and that he would never give a blind adherence or support to any party, whether in power or in opposition, at the dictation of any leader.

The Government of Sir John had been sustained at the polls, and when the House met in the spring of 1873, there was a majority of some forty-five members, which might be reckoned upon; and business of the House

went on smoothly until the Hon. Mr. Huntington's
famous notice of motion was given on the subject of
the " Pacific Scandal."

Parliament adjourned soon after the scandal was announced, and met again in October, to deliberate on the
evidence taken before a royal commission held in Montreal.   The result was the fall of the Conservative Ministry in the month of November, 1873.

The Hon. Alexander McKenzie, who had for some
years been the able leader of the Opposition, was sent
for by His Excellency the Governor-General, to form a
ministry.   This task he accomplished; and having closed
the more urgent business of the session, Parliament was
prorogued and shortly afterwards dissolved, and writs for
a general election issued.   This general election was held
in January, 1874, when Mr. Scatcherd was again the
chosen candidate to represent the North Riding.   No
opposition being offered from any quarter, he was returned by acclamation.

He had now been five several times chosen to serve his
country in her chief national council.   Thrice he succeeded against strong opposition, and twice unanimously
returned without a contest; thus proving that the longer
he was before the public, and the better they were able
to judge and scrutinize his political career, the more
firmly he took root in their confidence and esteem.

Once more he was called upon to resume his duties in Parliament, where his well-known reputation for ability, experience and impartiality caused his services to be sought for on various committees; thus adding greatly to the labors usually performed by members.

The session of the winter and spring of 1876 was a busy one; and, in defectively-ventilated chambers, poisoned by vitiated air, proved a severe tax upon the health of many of the members. The duties devolving upon Mr. Scatcherd were exceedingly onerous. In addition to his labors as a prominent member of several ordinary committees, he was appointed Chairman of the Committee of Supply. To those unacquainted with parliamentary routine, it may be explained that this is a committee of the whole House; the members not occupying a room apart in the day-time, like ordinary committees, but is in itself a sitting of the House. The Member for North Middlesex was for the time being Speaker. The sittings extended frequently until long after midnight, during which he would not leave the chair. It is, therefore, not surprising that the severe labor, together with interruption of the usual hours of rest required to recuperate exhausted strength, caused too great a strain upon his usually robust constitution. That he succumbed to the accumulated evil influence of overwork and an impure atmosphere, is, alas! only too true.

A strong personal friendship had grown up between Mr. Scatcherd and the Member for Kent, Mr. Rufus Stephenson. While taking a walk, they stood a few moments to observe the voting at an election then being held in Ottawa city. Mr. Stephenson, noticing that his friend looked unusually pale, remarked: " Scatcherd, do you feel ill? You look very pale." The reply was: "No; I never felt better in my life; let us finish our walk."

This was Saturday afternoon, April 1st. The following Monday, Mr. Scatcherd dined with Mr. Wright, one of the members. After dinner he went to the House, and took his seat as usual. He was observed to leave before adjournment, something uncommon with him. Immediately after reaching the hotel, he retired, and passed a very restless night. Early next morning he called Dr. Browse, who thought it a bilious attack. The prescription appeared not to have a beneficial effect. Other remedies were administered, but without any good result. His suffering in the meantime had become intense. Still, his condition was not considered alarming.

He did not wish to give his family any unnecessary uneasiness, and consequently did not communicate with them. On Thursday a consultation of medical men was held, and different treatment prescribed. At this time, although the symptoms were such as to excite some

degree of alarm, his case was not thought very danger-
ous. The medicines were useless. On Friday, there
being no indication of improvement, his family were
advised of his illness, and on Saturday sent for. Saturday, Sunday and Monday brought no change, except
for the worse, in the obstinacy of the disease.

On the morning of Tuesday the 12th his wife, son and
neice arrived and found him very low. Their presence
soothed and appeared to relieve him very much; he
seemed to rally, and partook of refreshments with relish.
The improvement did not continue long. It became
evident to all he was in a most critical condition. Much
had been expected from his strong and vigorous constitution; but nothing seemed to avail. On Thursday dispatches
were sent to his brother James and to his law-partner,
Mr. W. R. Meredith. They arrived on Friday. He was
greatly pleased to see them. His pleasure was expressed
more by a feeling of contentment and resignation than
by words. During the afternoon he felt better and was
able to stand up; asked for refreshments, partook of
them, and spoke of their tasting good. He turned himself unaided in bed, folded his arms, and fell into what
appeared a placid and refreshing sleep.

Those favorable indications raised the hopes of family
and friends, and led them to think and hope the crisis in
his disease had been reached and safely passed, notwithstanding the physicians had given him up. A sad disap-

pointment, however, was soon to be realized. From this sleep he did not again fully and clearly awake. When spoken to he appeared conscious of what was said, but did not speak in return. His right pulse was but slightly increased, while his left ran up to one hundred and thirty. At six o'clock it became painfully evident that all hope of recovery must be abandoned. He refused everything offered him, and only expressed recognition feebly by a nod of the head.

For the past three days he endured but little pain, and now the suffering had entirely ceased. The nature of his disease was such that it might be truthfully said he was really dying from the first day he was taken ill.

He now recognized those around him only by the voice, continuing to sink gradually and painlessly, until three o'clock on Saturday morning, fifteenth of April, when he calmly and quietly breathed his last.

Though far from the home he loved so well, he died surrounded by relatives and kind friends. Around his bedside were his wife, youngest son and niece; his brother James and wife; Mr. W. R. Meredith, his partner; his kind friends, Mr. Rufus Stephenson, Mr. Charles McIntosh, the Reverend Mr. Pollard, and others highly esteemed.

His son Ethel and the family physician, Dr. Woodruff of London, arrived only in time to take the returning train, which bore the remains to London; and his brother, R. C. Scatcherd of Strathroy, met the train near Kingston.

His dearly-beloved and heart-stricken wife, and relatives, will ever remember with gratitude the kindness and devotion of friends in Ottawa during his illness, who were constant throughout in their ministrations of tenderness and sympathy. And now in 1878:

To the Honorable Edward Blake, and to Mrs. Blake, who kindly tendered the use of their home, passed much of their valuable time, night and day, at his bedside, and from their table sent choicest delicacies:

To Messrs. Wright and Biggar, Members of Parliament, and M. C. McIntosh, for their kind and consoling attentions; and to Mr. Rufus Stephenson, who from the first was constant and unremitting in his attention and assistance, scarcely absenting himself from the bedside of the sufferer, weary and worn, waiting and watching over his friend with the kindness and tenderness of a brother, the gratitude of the family is again expressed, and here recorded.

If anything earthly could mitigate or soften the anguish of this painful affliction, it is the kindness and sympathy received, during the sad and trying hour of darkness and sorrow, from those named, and from others who, although not named here, are not forgotten.

From the commencement of his illness, Mr. Scatcherd had the best and most skillful treatment obtainable in

13

Ottawa. It is the opinion of those best able to judge, that from the first no skill could have availed against his disease (pyæmia) when manifesting itself in such malignant form and force in the beginning.

Alluding to the death of Mr. Scatcherd, the *Ottawa Citizen* said:

From the Ottawa Citizen, April 15, 1876.

This morning shortly after three o'clock, the hand of death removed Mr. Thomas Scatcherd, M. P. for North Middlesex, from amongst us. He passed away peacefully, surrounded by his family, after an illness of two weeks, during which his gradual decline was borne with Christian fortitude. The lamented gentleman was the eldest son of the late John Scatcherd, for many years Member for West Middlesex, who died in Toronto, in 1858, whilst attending to his parliamentary duties. In 1861 Mr. Thomas Scatcherd, then a rising barrister in London, took the field against Mr. A. P. Macdonald and the late Mr. James Keefer, being elected for his father's former constituency by a large majority. From the day he entered Parliament Mr. Scatcherd drew around him a large circle of friends. Possessed of a shrewd, practical mind, taking a liberal view of every question, his votes were recorded more in accordance with a sense of his responsibilities as a member than as the mere representative of a party. True to his friends as a politician, he still took higher grounds, and throughout his career endeavored to maintain his own reputation as one who believed in justice to his opponents, and one whose private integrity could not be used to cover political errors. Consequently, when next appealing to his constituents, he was returned by an immense majority, both political parties tendering him a most flattering support.

In 1867 the ridings of North and West Middlesex were re-distributed, Mr. Scatcherd decided to run for North Middlesex, and being returned by over eight hundred majority. During the debates he spoke very briefly, but upon the entrance of Sir Francis Hincks into the Administration of the day, delivered a forcible speech in the defense of that gentleman having published a circular addressed to the Reform party—using these words: "I think the Finance Minister had done more for Reform than probably any other man in the Dominion, and I cannot see that he exceeded his privileges in writing the circular * * * I intend to deal with the Government, and their measures as they are brought forward, and not with their actions in the past." We quote these words to show how liberal the lamented gentleman was in his views, and how true to the principles then enunciated he remained. Born a Reformer in the strictest acceptation of the term, he never flinched from condemning his party and opposing his leaders when their policy appeared inimical to the interests of the country or not in consonance with the views publicly expressed by him. To young members he was particularly courteous, but being free from ostentation, and contented to do his duty from a conscientious sense of responsibility, and not merely measuring his fealty to principle by prospective personal advantages to be derived from such a course, Mr. Scatcherd at times appeared indifferent either to eulogy or censure, and would say more in defense of a friend, or one whom he considered unfairly dealt with, than he ever attempted to say in defense of any policy adopted by him in public life, and which he conscientiously believed to be correct.

In 1872 the lamented gentleman again offered for North Middlesex, and despite the bitter partizanship that characterized the general election of that period, no candidate was found to oppose him and he was elected by acclamation. In 1874 the same constituency again honored him, without opposition, and during the past three sessions of the third Parliament of the Dominion, he was unremitting in his attention to parliamentary duties.. As Chairman of the Committee of Supply both sides of the House placed implicit confidence in him; and this session, up to the day upon which he was stricken down, he held that position; and even when complaining of depressed spirits and illness, still sat night after night until the house adjourned, and he could find short rest preparatory to discharging his duties as a member of the Standing ·Committees. Only a few weeks ago he was appointed a Queen's Counsel, and many looked forward to his speedy promotion either to a Cabinet or judicial position. Death, however, has overtaken one who could illy be spared either as a public man or private citizen. Those who knew him best will alone be able to estimate the loss. In no spirit of vain flattery to the one now beyond the reach of either praise or censure have we referred to his many virtues; years of intimate friendship—years during which both his private and political acts were carefully watched—convinced us that the man who has passed away was worthy of the high estimation in which all classes held him; worthy of the respect which he commanded from both political friends and opponents.

Mr. Scatcherd was approaching his fifty-third birthday when called to his long home. He died surrounded by his relatives, who hastened to his bedside so soon as the intelligence of his illness being serious reached them. As a husband he was ever attentive, generous and thoughtful; as a father, ever indulgent and considerate; and if the deep and sincere sympathy of the public can alleviate the affliction of a sorrowing family circle, then most assuredly that sympathy will be extended in all its abundance. The mortal remains of Mr. Scatcherd were taken from the Russell House this morning and conveyed to the St. Lawrence and Ottawa Railway, and left by the noon train for London. The pall-bearers were the Premier, Hon. A. Mackenzie; Hon. Edward Blake, Minister of Justice; Hon. A. J. Smith, Minister of Marine and Fisheries; Hon. Mr. Vail, Minister of Militia; Hon. J. W. Anglin, Speaker of the House of Commons; Mr. Rufus Stephenson, M. P., and Rev. Mr. Pollard. The Hon. Messrs. Scott, Laird, Burpee and Cauchon, also a large number of the citizens of Ottawa, were present to pay their last tribute of respect to the deceased. Special arrangements were made with the St. Lawrence and Ottawa, and Grand Trunk Railroads to convey the remains to Toronto, and a special train engaged there *via* Grand Trunk R. R. to London.

A meeting of the Bar of London was at once called for Monday, the 17th, at three P. M. Every member of the legal profession in the city was in attendance. Resolutions were carried, expressive of their grief, and of the great loss the profession had sustained by the loss of one of its oldest and most able members, and tendering their heartfelt sympathy to the widow and family of the deceased. And as an additional mark of respect for his memory, it was resolved that each member of the profession should wear a badge of mourning for the space of one month; also, that the resolutions should be engrossed on parchment, and inclosed to his bereaved family.

Similar meetings of both the Reform and Conservative associations of North Middlesex were held at Ailsa Craig, for the purpose of giving expression to their feelings. Resolutions of sympathy and condolence were unanimously passed, and forwarded to the family of their late member. In short, but one feeling pervaded the whole community, both far and near: a feeling that, as a citizen, as a professional man of high character and unbending integrity; and, above all, as a public character, representing the interests of his fellow-countrymen in the Legislature of the Dominion, it would be long indeed before they should see his like again.

The last token of respect which could be shown was in following his remains to their last resting-place. His funeral took place on the eighteenth of April, and was attended by over three thousand persons; while the closing of stores and suspension of business during the passage of the sad procession through the city, testified how general was the sentiment of sorrow.

Public opinion, both in Parliament and in the country, had already indicated him as the probable Government nominee for the Speakership of the Dominion House of Commons: a choice which would have been acquiesced in and approved of by all parties without distinction: a position which he would have filled with as much credit to himself as advantage to the country.

His well-trained judicial mind; his unswerving integrity, and his perfect freedom from political bias, eminently qualified him for the important position of First Commoner of Canada. A sound and able lawyer, well qualified for the discharge of judicial duties, advancement from the Speakership to a seat on the Bench of one of our Superior Courts would have been both a natural and a merited sequence: a choice which would have met the approval of the profession and the public, and have been justified by his great legal attainments, strict impartiality, and laborious discharge of important duties involved in high offices. But it has been decreed otherwise, and it becomes his loving friends to submit.

Mr. Scatcherd at his death left a devoted wife and two sons to mourn his loss, Ethelwolf and Henry Sandwith, aged respectively twenty-one and nineteen.

He also left three brothers and four sisters. His brothers are: James N., a successful merchant in the city of Buffalo for many years; Robert Colin, a well-known legal practitioner in the town of Strathroy, three times elected Mayor of the municipality—he succeeded the deceased member in the parliamentary representation of North Middlesex; and George, extensively engaged in agricultural pursuits in Nissouri. His sisters are: Jane, Lavinia, Anne, and Mary. They were a most united family, and the deceased being the eldest, was looked up to as head and guide; and never was a brother more truly a brother than Thomas. In all that pertained to the welfare and happiness of each member of the family his solicitude was unbounded. He was the center of their affections, and to them a dearly beloved brother.

Of Mr. Robert Colin Scatcherd, this further notice claims a place.

THE MEMBER FOR NORTH MIDDLESEX.—The Ottawa correspondent of Hamilton *Times* gives the following sketch of Robert Colin Scatcherd, member of the House of Commons for North Middlesex:

"It will be recollected when Parliament was prorogued last April, that among the members absent was Mr. Thomas Scatcherd, Q. C., M. P. for North Middlesex and City Solicitor for London. He had been missing from his seat in the front row of ministerial benches for several days, owing to an illness he had, beyond a doubt, contracted from sitting during long hours, night after night, as Chairman of the Committee of Supply—a position of such importance that the gentleman selected to fill it is generally one of large parliamentary experience, and one who, as time passes, comes to be regarded as a likely candidate for further government honors. For several sessions, Mr. Scatcherd had managed the committee with great acceptability. He was a favorite with gentlemen on both sides of the House, being sincere and straightforward in his conversation, pithy in his generally too infrequent speeches, genial in his manner, and ever striving to be impartial in judgment. His lamented death occurred at the Russell House almost immediately after Parliament was prorogued, and, of course, a vacancy was created in North Middlesex, which he had satisfactorily represented for many years—in fact ever since the death of his father, Mr. John Scatcherd, who, like himself, died at his post, attending to his parliamentary duties. The death of the latter occurred in Toronto in 1858. The new representative of North Middlesex is a son of the late Mr. John Scatcherd, and, of course, a brother of the late Mr. Thomas Scatcherd; his name is Robert Colin Scatcherd. The present member, to an almost remarkable degree, resembles his late brother, the chief difference, perhaps, consisting of the fact that he is younger in appearance. He seems also to be very similar in his disposition, being rather reticent in manner, yet friendly, and very well liked. He is rapidly filling the void created by the decease of his brother, and doubtless, in time, will come to be as highly esteemed. He has not yet addressed the House, but will probably make his maiden speech this session. Mr. Scatcherd was born in London, Ont., on the twelfth of November, 1832, and has practiced law at Strathroy since 1863. He was Mayor of Strathroy for three successive years, until June 7, 1876, when he was elected to Parliament. He is a Liberal, and, of course, a supporter of the Government."

As might be expected from his prudent habits and large practice, Mr. Thomas Scatcherd left his family in quite independent circumstances.

He frequently visited the old homestead, which belonged to him at the time of his death; and never felt happier than when contemplating the scenes of his birth and childhood, and more mature youth. And had it pleased God to have spared his life to a green old age, it is not improbable that he would have taken refuge from the toils and labors of life in the seclusion of his early home, enjoying the social intercourse of beloved relatives and attached friends.

Those visits to the farm are sweetly remembered in household memories. The excursions were pleasant diversions from city life and business, to enjoy the pure country air amidst scenes domestically sanctified. Rarely did he go to Wyton woods and cultured fields without bringing from the forest a shrub to be transplanted in his garden. He seemed to have no choice as to any particular kind, but selected some weak or sickly plant struggling for existence with poor chances of success. Gently and tenderly it was removed and transferred to his garden, there to be watched over and cared for with solicitude until it was either able to take care of itself or died. A sturdy grape-vine in the garden was, when brought from its native forest, a puny, sickly shoot. It now overshadows a large tree of his own planting, and is strangling it with too much friendship in a constantly-extending embrace.

The garden, in varieties represented, is a miniature forest: ferns, bloodroot, mandrakes, crowfoot, leeks and many others of similar kinds; some, perhaps, unknown as to class or family. Gooseberry, wild current, cranberry and dogwood bushes, along with basswood, beech, maple, oak and pine, were planted promiscuously. When they grew a little they were too dense to thrive; and although many of them died, no amount of argument could induce him to thin out or trim them. His reply was, " I have given them all a fair start, and an equal chance; now let them take care of themselves."

Such phrases of common-place sentiment found utterance when drawn from his lips by the kindly suggestiveness of transient associates. But in the mental depths of Thomas Scatcherd's nature, the silent affections were awakened in presence of the miniature forest. Sympathy pervaded his spiritual being as a fragrant perfume; too indistinct for shaping into words; too sweetly per-

sonal and precious for a conversational social atmosphere.
At sight of the garden thickets his soul was in Wyton
woodlands; not as they are now ornamentally sheltering
and adorning the cultured fields of bountiful harvests,
but as they were. He journeyed from city offices and
crowded law courts for country air, and also for the
atmosphere of sentiment. His mother planted a walnut,
the nut became a plant, the plant a tree; this is the tree.
His father planted those tall pines, and himself the rows
of poplars now in maturity. There is the spot in the
green meadow, on the bank of the wimpling Wye, where
stood the log-house of his parents in years of early
housekeeping. And there he first heard of Heaven,
looking in his mother's eyes lisping his infant prayer.

The miniature forest in the London city garden was
a sanctuary to the intellectual man. The plants spoke
a language interpreted only in his own psychological
being.

In a previous chapter, one who was a pupil in Miss
Stimson's school relates the sweet incident of the boy
Thomas Scatcherd entering for the first time, and, under
influence of the sentiments and training of his pious
mother and father, advancing straight to a seat, where,
kneeling down in the presence of the assembled pupils,
but heeding not them, addressed himself in prayer to
God the Father and to Christ the Redeemer, who said:

" Suffer little children to come unto me, and forbid them not: for of such is the Kingdom of Heaven."

The pupil who told this, and described the primitive London school-room, was in after-life the Reverend Elam Stimson—nephew of the lady-teacher—a clergyman of the English Episcopal Church. In a letter he says:

"After the period of early pupilage, our pursuits were cast in different lines, and we met occasionally in advanced boyhood, only to compare notes in accessions of elementary knowledge. Subsequently to this, on his way to Parliament, we sometimes had an opportunity of referring to past and present.

" His life terminated almost in my presence. Being at the Russell House at Ottawa during two of his last days, it came to my knowledge that he was not likely to recover from his prostration. It was too late to press such attentions as I could command, when others especially were there who knew how to proffer those services which might prove the most acceptable to him. My sympathies, though, could find relief in the reflection that the beginning and the end of Thomas Scatcherd's life became known to me in the manner described; and that, as prayerful devotions characterized the opening of his career in the world, so his manhood was not without usefulness and success, and his last hours those of peace here, and assurance of happiness hereafter."

CHAPTER X.

From the Ottawa Times, April 15, 1876.

Morning Edition: We regret to learn that Mr. Scatcherd, M. P., at a late hour last night was in an extremely low condition, and very serious doubts were expressed by his medical attendants as to whether he would last until morning. Some of his relatives arrived yesterday, but he was scarcely able to recognize them. He became insensible at five o'clock in the evening, and remained in the same state up to the time of writing.

Evening Edition: The session of 1876 closes mournfully. When the first side of the *Times* went to press this morning, there appeared, as we stated, reason to fear that the name of Mr. Scatcherd would be struck from the parliamentary roll by the inexorable hand of Death. The apprehension, we regret to learn, was verified at twenty minutes past three this morning. His many friends will hear of his decease and will sympathize with us in the pain with which we make the announcement.

From the Montreal Witness, April 15, 1876.

OTTAWA, April 15.—The death of Mr. Scatcherd has cast a gloom over this city, where he was widely known and highly respected. He was taken ill about two weeks ago, after sitting for a great many hours as Chairman of the Committee of Supply in the House of Commons. At first it was only considered a bilious attack, but soon developed into pyæmia, or blood poisoning, which attacked the brain. His stomach would retain nothing, and his system sank for want of nourishment. Dr. Brouse, M. P., attended him, and also Drs. Grant and Carmichael, but all their skill was in vain. He rallied occasionally till the night before last, when all hope was abandoned. Quietly and peacefully he passed away at a quarter past three o'clock this morning. At the time of his death there were with him his wife and niece, his brother James and wife, his younger son, his law-partner, Mr. Meredith, and Rufus Stephenson, the last-mentioned of whom attended him since he was taken down with a devotion that deserves the highest praise. He died at the Russell House, where every possible care and attention was shown him. Some time ago Mr. Blake placed his residence at the sick man's disposal, but it was found impossible to remove him from the hotel. His partner, Mr. Meredith, arrived yesterday morning and his elder son this morning, the latter unfortunately too late to see his father alive. Rev. Mr. Pollard attended him in his last moments. The friends of the deceased having determined to remove the remains to his home in London, special arrangements were made with the St. Lawrence and Ottawa Railway, and the funeral left the Russell House at ten o'clock this A. M., and left Ottawa by the usual morning train. The pall-bearers were the Hons. A. Mackenzie, E. Blake, A. J. Smith, T. W. Anglin, Vail, and R. Stephenson, M. P. All the other members of the Cabinet and those members of Senate and Commons in town, with a number of private citizens, attended the funeral. Arrangements have been made for a special train to convey the remains from Toronto to London. Doubtless the questionable system of forcing the work of the session through in nine or ten weeks has had its share in causing the ill health amongst members of the Commons, reporters and officers of Parliament. It is hinted that the indemnity allowed members should enable them to give an extra week or so for the transaction of public business.

From the Montreal Witness (Editorial) same date.

By the death of Mr. Scatcherd, of London, the late Member for North Middlesex, the Canadian House of Commons has lost one of its most useful private members. He was an able man, but there are many able Commoners, and his ability is not what will be chiefly missed. The qualities which will render it difficult to fill his place, were his clear-headedness and perfect impartiality with the thorough control which he had over his temper. When he was in his place, he was always made Chairman of the Committee of Supply, and the even way in which he held the scales of justice in deciding points of order, in this most important committee, where the fiercest party fights often take place, won for him deep respect from both sides of the House. No complaint of party unfairness on his part was ever made, and once last session when roundly abused by a prominent member, who did not hear it read, although his leader had assented to the item passing, he did not permit the slightest sign of any resentment at this extemely unfair criticism. By profession he was a lawyer, and last session he was Chairman of the Standing Committee of Privileges and Elections. Mr. Scatcherd was a native of the county of Middlesex, part of which he continually represented in the old Canadian Assembly, and afterwards in the House of Commons, since 1861. He was born in 1823, being about fifty-two years of age at the time of his death.

From the Montreal Evening Star, April 17 (Conservative Journal).

THE LATE THOMAS SCATCHERD, M. P.—North Middlesex, Ont., has lost a trusty representative in the person of Thomas Scatcherd, Esq., M. P., whose death was announced from Ottawa on Saturday. He has fallen a victim, we fear, to the poisonous air of the Parliament buildings, whose foulness has told upon the constitution of more than one legislator and journalist during the session which has just expired. Called away in the

prime of a vigorous life—he was but fifty-two—he leaves a gap
in the representation of the important constituency of North
Middlesex which will not be speedily filled again. Mr.
Scatcherd may be said to have succeeded his father as member
for the county. John Scatcherd emigrated from Yorkshire in
1821, and settled in West Middlesex, where Thomas was born,
at Wyton, Nissouri, in 1823. The father sat for the county in
the Canadian Assembly up to the time of his death in 1858;
Thomas, the son, was elected in 1861 and sat until Confederation. He was educated at the London Grammar School, and
early entered upon the study of law. He was called to the
Bar of Upper Canada in Hilary Term, 1848, and in 1851 he
married Miss Isabella Sprague, of Yarmouth, a grand-daughter
of the late Elias Moore, who represented Middlesex in the
Upper Canada Assembly. Mr. Scatcherd was returned by
acclamation at every successive election since Confederation,
his constituents having unbounded confidence in his integrity.
In politics he was a Liberal, and a supporter of the Government of Mr. Mackenzie. Personally, he was a man of sterling
character and high intelligence. An active parliamentarian,
he took but little part in debate, preferring solid work to tor-
rents of words, but when he spoke he commanded an influence
much greater than that of many men with whose names the public have been made far more widely familiar. He had no greed
of political advancement. While men with but a tittle of his service and experience have acceded to high office in the State,
he was content to remain in the ranks and serve his constituency faithfully as a private member. Middlesex in him loses a
faithful representative, and the Dominion a worthy and distinguished public man.

From the Montreal Herald, April 17, 1876.

THE LATE THOMAS SCATCHERD, M. P.—The death of Mr.
Scatcherd, late Member for North Middlesex, which took place

in Ottawa on Saturday morning last, causes a real loss to the body of which he was a member, and the constituency that he represented. He was an admirable example of that class of men who, though the outside public know but little of them as in proportion to their merits, nevertheless have a weight and value in the House that is not attained by many of those whom the *Hansard* has delighted to honor. The son of the late John Scatcherd, Esq., himself for some time the representative of West Middlesex in the Canadian Assembly, and a well-known figure for many years in Upper Canadian politics, Mr. Scatcherd had been in political life since 1861. Able, clear-headed, and impartial, he was the almost invariable Chairman of the Committee of Supply, and there can be no doubt that the severity of his labors in connection with this position, did much to sow the seeds of the disease to which he succumbed. It was hoped until the other day that his illness was not of a serious nature, and it was only for a day or two before his death that the gravity of his situation was realized. He was greatly liked and respected by all with whom he came in contact, both on account of his ability and his character; and his death is a severe blow to his many friends.

From the Montreal Gazette, April 17 (leading Conservative Paper).

DEATH OF MR. SCATCHERD, M. P.—We deeply regret to chronicle the death of Mr. Thomas Scatcherd, the Member for North Middlesex, which took place at the Russell House, Ottawa, on Saturday morning. Mr. Scatcherd was taken ill about a fortnight ago with what was thought to be a severe attack of bilious fever. For the first three or four days of his illness he suffered most severely, getting literally no sleep, and being unable to retain any food. Dr. Brouse, who was in constant attendance upon him, then regarded him as in a fair way of recovering, and, although he was very weak, no serious apprehensions for him were entertained. As his recovery was so

14

slow, however, it was deemed prudent to send for Mrs. Scatcherd, who, with her niece, arrived in Ottawa on Tuesday last. Finding the patient so very feeble, it was decided to send for his brother and other relatives, among them his son, who, however, arrived too late to see him alive. During the latter part of the week he sank rapidly, and, after some hours of unconsciousness, passed away on Saturday morning.

Mr. Scatcherd was elected for the West Riding of Middlesex at the election of 1861, and has since represented the North Riding in the Commons of Canada. He was a native of the county, having been born at Wyton, township of Nissouri, in 1823. His father represented the West Riding of the county in the old Parliament of Canada. He was a man of good though not showy abilities, and of very sterling common sense. He seldom took part in the debates of Parliament, although when he did so, he spoke tersely and to the point, and was always well listened to. For some years past he has been the Chairman of the Committee of Supply, and his illness is attributed in part to the labor this position involved, especially during the absurdly long sittings which Mr. Mackenzie insisted on forcing upon members. In his last illness he was attended with unremitting care by Mr. Rufus Stephenson, the Member for Kent, who remained over after the adjournment in order to watch by his bed-side. The funeral took place from Ottawa on Saturday morning, the body being conveyed to London, where it will be interred.

From the Hamilton Times.

MR. SCATCHERD, than whom there were few, if any, more conscientious and hard-working members in the House, was unremitting in his attendance. Being well versed in the rules of debate, and on points of order, he was nearly always called to the chair when the House was in committee upon important legal measures, or in Committee of Supply, where he alone shared the duties with Mr. Young, of Waterloo, who in Mr. Scatcherd's absence presided altogether. By his death the House will sustain an almost irreparable loss. His ability, fairness, assiduity and genial disposition made him one of the most respected and popular members in Parliament, and the illness of no one caused more regret than his.

From the Toronto Mail.

MR. SCATCHERD had been in Parliament from 1861 to the time of his death. A steady adherent of the Reform side of politics, he was a useful man to his party in the House of which he was a member. He rarely spoke at much length, but he invariably spoke in a way to command attention, because of the excellent common sense, which dictated his utterances. As Chairman of the Committee of Supply for several years he did good service. Though of quiet and unobtrusive habits, he made many friends and was universally liked and respected.

From the Toronto Globe.

HE was known as a most efficient member of the House of Commons, and had, since the present Government came into office, usually occupied the chair in Committee of Supply, while on other occasions his sound judgment and practical knowledge caused his services in the Select and Standing Committees of the House to be frequently called into requisition. He was not a frequent speaker, and seldom on the floor for more than a few minutes at a time, but his remarks were always shrewd and to the point, and listened to with the greatest respect. Although a firm supporter of the Government, he was accustomed to express his views with much frankness and independence. Beneath a somewhat reserved manner might be discovered a kind and genial nature, and a strong sense of justice in his relation to those with whom in his parliamentary career he was brought into contact. With him a good and useful man has passed away, leaving, it may safely be said, in the constituency he represented and the assembly to which he belonged, not one who would begrudge this tribute due to his memory.

From the London Advertiser.

DEATH OF MR. SCATCHERD, M. P.—The general public of Ontario, and more particularly that portion of it residing in London and the west, learned with much concern that Mr. Thomas Scatcherd, M. P., had been lying seriously ill at Ottawa for some time past. The reports received from day to day, led to an alternation between hope and fear on his account, but it at last became evident to most that a fatal weakness had set in. It is now our painful duty to record his death, which took place peacefully on Saturday, at three o'clock A. M. At the time of his decease he was surrounded by his family and many personal friends, including his partner, Mr. Meredith, Mr. Rufus Stephenson and others. Everything had been done for him which medical skill and individual solicitude could devise, but without permanent avail. Mr. Scatcherd was eminently a London man. Born not many miles distant, at Wyton, in November, 1823; he finished his education at the London District Grammar School, and was called to the Bar in 1848. Soon after, he entered into a partnership in his profession with Mr. E. J. Parke, which continued successfully for some time. Subsequently, he pursued business on his own account, and for some years past in association with Mr. William Meredith, M. P. P., and acted for a considerable period as City Solicitor. In 1851 he married Miss Isabella Sprague, of Yarmouth. His father, Mr. John Scatcherd—who emigrated to Canada in 1821—was elected to represent the important riding of West Middlesex in Parliament of United Canada in 1854, but dying soon after, was succeeded in the representation by his son Thomas. Upon the re-division of the county for electoral purposes, he was invited to contest the North Riding, which he did successfully in 1867, and carried the constituency by acclamation in 1872, and again at the last general election in 1874.

Mr. Scatcherd's political affinities were with what is known as the Reform party, but he had the good-will of men of all parties. He was not an extremist in anything, but held a well-balanced judgment upon all affairs. Within the walls of Parliament no one has been more respected, and his name has often been advanced as that of one whose position and services entitled him to a seat in the Government of the country. He was always a hard worker on important committees, and as Chairman of the Committee of the Whole during some sessions past, won general approval by his assiduity, his fairness and thorough knowledge of affairs brought under notice. Though he could not be said to be a leading speaker in the House, yet when he did rise to his feet, he had always something to say that was worth listening to, and his eloquence, though unadorned, was none the less convincing. In his efforts before juries, he displayed the faculty of keeping his language within the comprehension of those whom he was called upon to address, and by the simplicity of his style and sincerity of purpose, attained the position of a favorite pleader at the London Bar. In his social capacity he was much esteemed. Everybody had a good word for Mr. Scatcherd, and though in his professional as his political capacity, he was obliged to come in adverse contact with many interests, he has passed away without leaving an enemy behind him. Among the principal features in his character which contributed to his success, was a perfect trustworthiness in all his transactions, a probity and candor which were never found lacking. His decease in the fifty-third year of his age, is deeply regretted by a very large circle of friends, and will leave a painful gap in that community of citizenship, which dates in London from the day of small things up to the present prosperous condition of affairs. The remains of Mr. Scatcherd will be attended to their last resting-place by a very numerous retinue of sorrowing friends and acquaintances.

From the London Daily Advertiser.

The Bar, Board of Education and City Council Express Condolence.—The universal regret felt by all classes of the community over the death of the late Thomas Scatcherd, Esq., is the best index of the esteem in which that gentleman was held during a long residence in London. He had grown up with the city, and had seen it rise from an obscure place in the wilderness to a thriving commercial center. His heartfelt desire was to witness London advance, and become what nature has intended it should be, the leading city of Western Ontario. As a professional man he was most widely known and respected hereabouts, and in West and North Middlesex in the capacity of politician the deceased was looked up to as a gentleman whose advice was worth procuring. No wonder then that sympathy of the sincerest kind should be shared by a large class of people, on the occasion of his death. The funeral, which has been arranged to take place from his late residence, Dundas street east, at three o'clock this afternoon, to St. Paul's Cathedral Cemetery, London East, will, we feel sure, bear out the remarks made above, both as regards numbers and respectability. The members of the Bar, the School Trustees, the Board of Aldermen, the Police Force and the Fire Department, in addition to very large deputations from the townships surrounding this city, together with citizens generally, will attend the obsequies of the deceased, which are to take place punctually at the hour named. On the plate of the metallic coffin is engraved, "T. Scatcherd, aged fifty-two years; died April 15th, 1876." The pall-bearers on the occasion will comprise many of Mr. Scatcherd's warmest friends, namely, Messrs.

J. C. Meredith, E. W. Hyman, E. Leonard, Hon. John
Carling, V. Cronyn, W. Horton, George Webster, S. H. Gray-
don, M. Macintyre (West Williams), and John Flanigan
(McGillivray).

Action of the London Bar.

AT three o'clock yesterday afternoon, and for the first time
in twenty years, the members of the Bar of London met at the
court-house to express regret at the death of one of their
number, and he the late Thomas Scatcherd, Q. C., who died
in Ottawa, at an early hour on Saturday morning last.   There
were in attendance, Messrs. W. Horton; E. J. Parke; James
Shanly; C. D. Holmes; H. Macmahon, Q. C.; W. C. L. Gill;
T. Partridge; V. Cronyn; B. Cronyn; T. O'Brien; R. Bayly;
J. H. Fraser, M. P.; D. McMillan, M. P.; E. Meredith;
M. D. Fraser; E. R. Reid; C. Hutchinson; A. Greenlees;
C. Goodhue; John Macbeth; J. Martin; C. S. Corrigan;
J. R. Dixon; John Taylor; H. Becher; W. H. Bartram; Geo.
McNab, and others.

On motion, Col. Shanly was elected Chairman and Col.
Macbeth Secretary.

The Chairman, in opening the meeting, referred to the
purpose for which the meeting had been called—to express
their sorrow at the death of our late brother, Mr. Scatcherd,
a gentleman who was, during a long professional career
deservedly esteemed and respected by all with whom he
had professional intercourse.   It was for the meeting to take
whatever action might be deemed best to carry out the object
for which the members of the Bar had been called together.
Before resuming his seat he read the following note from His
Honor Judge Elliot:

My Dear Sir: I should like to join in any expression of regret on the
occasion of the removal from amongst us of one so much esteemed as the
late Mr. Scatcherd. If, as I hear, there is to be a meeting of the Bar

to-day for this, or for a kindred object, may I trouble you to give expression of my heartfelt sympathy and concurrence with it.

Believe me, yours sincerely,

WILLIAM ELLIOT.

LONDON, *April 17, 1876.*

Mr. C. D. Holmes then moved, seconded by Mr. H. Macmahon, Q. C., that Messrs. Flock, Bayly, Horton, J. H. Fraser, the Chairman and the mover be a committee to draft resolutions (and prepare a programme) suitable to the occasion.

The Committee presented the following resolutions :

WHEREAS, We, the Members of the Bar of Middlesex, have heard the announcement of the death of our brother, the late Thomas Scatcherd, Esq., Q. C., with feelings of the deepest regret, and with the most painful sense of the loss the profession has sustained in his sudden and unexpected removal from amongst us.

Resolved : That we attend the funeral of our deceased brother in a body, in our robes, and that we wear a badge of mourning for thirty days as a testimony of the profound respect which we entertain for his memory.

Resolved : That while in common with the public generally we deplore the death of our late brother and feel that he will long continue to occupy an affectionate place in our hearts, we desire in an especial manner to tender to Mrs. Scatcherd, her children and the relatives of the deceased, our most heartfelt sympathy in this their great bereavement and affliction.

Resolved : That the foregoing resolutions be engrossed on parchment and forwarded to Mrs. Scatcherd by the Chairman.

Mr. Macmahon moved, seconded by Mr. M. D. Fraser, the adoption of the above resolutions.

Mr. W. Horton said he desired to make a few remarks. When we last met here some three weeks since, I little imagined we would be called together upon such an occasion as this. I have known Mr. Scatcherd longer than any other member of the Bar in London, and for no member did I entertain more respect and esteem than for him. Whether in a public or private capacity our late brother was invariably guided by honorable motives, and I feel that in his death I have lost a warm and sincere friend. I am sure that every member of the Bar will join with me in feelings of regret, and extend our sincerest sympathy to the bereaved family.

Mr. Shanly felt sure that the sentiments uttered by his old friend Mr. Horton, would find a hearty response in the hearts of all present, and he could, on his part, but echo them.

Mr. Flock then moved, seconded by Mr. Taylor, that the members of the Bar meet at the office of Messrs. Macmahon, Gibbons & McNab, to-morrow (Tuesday) afternoon, at 2.30 o'clock, and then proceed in a body to the late residence of deceased.

Action of the Board of Education.

THE Board of Education met in the Clerk's office at 4.30.

There were present—Messrs. Cronyn (Chairman), Moffat, Reid, Wright, Orvell, Bayly, Cousins, Plummer, Miller, Sharman, Craig, Johnston, Shaw, McIntosh, Reed, Wilson.

The Chairman said he had called the members of the Board together in order that they might have an opportunity of recording their sense of loss, in what must be to them, as it was to the city and to the country generally, a sad affair, and of paying a tribute to one whom they all so much respected. Although not a member of this Board, Mr. Scatcherd had acted as its solicitor for many years, and he believed the members of the Board individually had found in the deceased gentleman a true friend. The Chairman then referred to his personal friendship with the deceased, stating that for the last few years he had been much thrown in contact with Mr. Scatcherd, and could bear testimony to his urbanity of character, and to his many kind and sympathetic acts in private life as well as to his upright public conduct.

Mr. Wright moved, and Mr. Reid seconded, that the following gentlemen form a committee to draft resolutions in reference to the object for which the Board had met: The Chairman, Messrs. Moffat and Bayly.

Mr. Reid claimed twenty-five years acquaintanceship with the deceased, and held the city and country generally had sustained a severe loss. He coincided in all the Chairman had said, and feeling this was not an occasion for much speaking, refrained from saying more.

The Committee having returned with the resolutions, they were moved as follows:

Moved by Mr. Alex. Johnson, seconded by Mr. Plummer, that the members of the Board of Education desire to join in the general feeling of sorrow occasioned by the death of Thomas Scatcherd, Esq., one of our most highly esteemed and respected citizens, and to record their deep sense of the loss which our city and country has sustained in the removal of one who in public as well as in private life was so much respected and esteemed, and they would express their sympathy with the family in their affliction.

Moved by Mr. Reid, seconded by Mr. Cousins, that out of respect to the memory of the late Mr. Scatcherd, the members of this Board attend his funeral to-morrow, in a body, and that a copy of the foregoing resolutions be forwarded to Mrs. Scatcherd, by the Chairman.

It is understood that the members of the Board (except those connected with the Bar) will meet in the City Hall, this afternoon, at half past two and proceed with the City Council to the residence of the deceased.

Action of the Board of Aldermen.

THE Board of Aldermen met in the City Clerk's office, last evening. His Worship The Mayor, presiding, and present: Aldermen Rapley, Skinner, Partridge, Sen., Minhinnick, Mc-

Phail, Christie, Hiscox, Williams, McColl, Campbell, Pritchard, Brown, Lewis, Fitzgerald, Thompson and Ross.

The Mayor, before proceeding with business, said it was his painful duty to inform the members—as no doubt they were aware of the fact—of the death of our valued servant, Thomas Scatcherd, Esq., for many years past our respected City Solicitor. He believed it was customary on occasions of this kind, out of respect to departed worth, to move resolutions of condolence with the family of bereaved ones, and he was ready now to receive a resolution of that character.

Alderman Campbell then arose and moved :

That this Council, having heard with feelings of extreme regret of the death of Thomas Scatcherd, Esq., M. P., which occurred while attending to his parliamentary duties in Ottawa ; be it, therefore,

Resolved : That we hereby express our deep sorrow at his sudden and unexpected removal, and our high appreciation of his long and valuable services as City Solicitor and legal adviser, as well as our heartfelt sympathy for his bereaved wife and family in their affliction, and that, as a tribute of respect to his memory, we do now adjourn, to meet here at 2.30 P. M., to-morrow, as a corporation, and attend the funeral of our deceased friend at the appointed hour, and that a copy of this resolution be engrossed and sent to his family.

Alderman Campbell, in speaking to the resolution said, when it was known that the late Mr. Scatcherd could not recover, a veritable gloom was cast over the city, and not a house in town but the members thereof felt that a good man had been removed from amongst us. As a professional man, Mr. Scatcherd was universally respected, and as a Canadian, he was an honor to his country. During his term of office he had given the city sound, honest advice, and although it may not have been to our liking at times, still we knew that we were advised by an honest man. He was sure that but one feeling pervaded all classes, and that was one of universal regret at the death of an esteemed citizen, who could be approached by any one, no matter what his position in life.

Alderman Fitzgerald seconded the resolution.

After instructing Captain Wigmore, Chief of Police, to make the usual arrangements, the Council adjourned to meet at the call of the Mayor.

It only remains to be said, that if these pages should be the means of inducing others to emulate the virtues, to walk in the footsteps, or to become aroused by the example of THOMAS SCATCHERD, the labor bestowed in this attempt to delineate his useful and honorable life will be fully requited.

The author would express his indebtedness to Mr. Alexander Somerville of Toronto, for valuable contributions, and for his assistance in carrying this volume through the press.

FAMILY RECORD.

Family Record.

THOMAS SCATCHERD'S CHILDREN.

Born in Beverley and Wyton, Yorkshire, England.

EMILY SCATCHERD, ... May 6, 1788

LAVINIA SCATCHERD, ... June 12, 1791

JAMES NEWTON SCATCHERD, . . Feb. 6, 1793

THOMAS SCATCHERD, ... April 12, 1795

JANE SCATCHERD, ... June 18, 1796

MARY SCATCHERD, ... Aug. 20, 1797

THOMAS SCATCHERD, ... Jan. 21, 1800

JOHN SCATCHERD, ... Jan. 21, 1800

THOMAS SCATCHERD, ... April 30, 1802

ANNE SCATCHERD, ... April 30, 1802

Family Record.

JOHN SCATCHERD'S CHILDREN.

Born in Canada.

Born in Wyton.

THOMAS SCATCHERD, ... Nov. 10, 1823

JAMES NEWTON SCATCHERD, . . Dec. 4, 1824

EMILY SCATCHERD, ... Sept. 24, 1826

JOHN SCATCHERD, ... July 22, 1828

JANE SCATCHERD, ... Aug. 3, 1830

Born in London.

ROBERT COLIN SCATCHERD, . . . Nov. 12, 1832

GEORGE SCATCHERD, ... Feb. 12, 1835

Born in Wyton.

WILLIAM SCATCHERD, ... Jan. 22, 1837

LAVINIA SCATCHERD, ... March 5, 1839

ANNE SCATCHERD, ... Jan. 22, 1841

MARY ELEANOR SCATCHERD, . . June 18, 1843

HARRY NEWTON SCATCHERD, . . Aug. 3, 1845

Family Record.

THOMAS SCATCHERD'S CHILDREN.

Born at Terrace Bank, Canada.

John Scatcherd, ...	Nov.	16,	1824
Foster Scatcherd, ...	Feb.	24,	1826
Anne Scatcherd, ...	Aug.	22,	1827
James Farley Scatcherd, . .	May	10,	1829
Thomas Scatcherd, ...	Jan.	11,	1830
Turner Scatcherd, ...	Jan.	11,	1830
Thomas Scatcherd, ...	Dec.	18,	1831
Mary Scatcherd, ...	Dec.	1,	1833
Jane Scatcherd, ...	Dec.	14,	1835
William Bailey Scatcherd, .	Jan.	7,	1838
Emily Charlotte Scatcherd,	Dec.	3,	1840
Lavinia Scatcherd, ...	March	11,	1842
Lavinia Scatcherd, ...	July	12,	1843
Lavinia Amelia Scatcherd, .	April	29,	1845
Edwin Scatcherd, ...	July	18,	1847
George Turner Scatcherd, .	Aug.	6,	1849
Harry Newton Scatcherd, .	Dec.	6,	1853

Family Record.

JOHN FARLEY'S CHILDREN.

Born in Armagh, Ireland.

ANNE FARLEY, ... Sept. 16, 1802

JAMES FARLEY, ... Dec. 17, 1804

JANE FARLEY, ... Jan. 27, 1806

TURNER FARLEY, ... Sept. 17, 1810